The Happy Hollisters at Circus Island

BY JERRY WEST

Illustrated by Helen S. Hamilton

GARDEN CITY, N.Y.

Doubleday & Company, Inc.

Contents

CHAPTER 1

A Dog Show

TWELVE-YEAR-OLD Pete Hollister bolted out of the
front door of his home, pulling a cap over his
blond crew-cut hair. As he hurried down the porch
steps of the large, rambling house, he almost ran
into his father.

"Whoa!" commanded Mr. Hollister with a
laugh.

The boy came to a sudden stop, sitting down
hard on the bottom step.

"Hi, Dad! How come you're home so early in
the afternoon?"

Mr. Hollister chuckled and put an arm about
Pete's shoulder. "Gather the clan together and I'll
tell you the secret that brought me home so early,"
he said.

Pete did an excellent roundup, and within ten
minutes the entire family, including Zip, their
collie dog, was in the pleasant living room, where a
fire burned merrily on the hearth.

There was Pam, a lovely ten-year-old girl with
golden-blonde hair and brown eyes. Then came
Ricky, who, at seven, was the daredevil of the family. His freckled face and reddish hair were as likely
to be seen upside down as right side up.

Next to this lively lad sat six-year-old Holly. Her brown pigtails fairly quivered with eagerness as she awaited the important news of the day, and her cheeks were red as the apple she held in her hand.

Last and littlest of all was Sue, who had come into the room with her attractive blonde mother. Climbing onto her father's knees, she put her arms around his neck as he began to speak.

"Well, Happy Hollisters," he began, "it looks as though your February vacation from school might be very extra-special this year."

"Oh, tell us!" Holly begged.

"How would all of you like to spend your vacation in Florida?" he asked.

"Florida!" five excited voices exclaimed as one.

Mrs. Hollister was as surprised as the four oldest children. Sue, however, did not seem to understand and asked her father, "What's Fourda? How does you spend it?"

Pete answered her quickly. "It's a place 'way down South where it's summer all the time," he explained, and then added; "boy, that sounds super, Dad. But what's the story?"

"A customer of mine wants to buy a houseboat and he'll pay a fine price to get a good one. He's been advertising in out-of-town papers and making inquiries everywhere, but so far he hasn't had any luck.

"This afternoon he had a letter from a man who has a houseboat to sell. This man's a clown with

6

the Sunshine Circus on Circus Island in Florida. My customer can't get away from business right now, so he has asked me to fly down there and have a look at the boat. How'd you all like to go along?"

"Yikes! Swell! Wonderful! Goody, goody! Hurray!"

The entire family chorused its delight in the proposal. Then Pam asked how soon they would go. Learning that her father had Friday in mind, she said, "Oh, Dad, that's the day of the dog show, remember? We've entered Zip in the Children's Class."

"Of course we'll wait until after the show. I'd almost forgotten," answered Mr. Hollister. "After all, it comes only once a year. I'll try to get plane reservations for Saturday morning."

Mrs. Hollister jumped to her feet. Her eyes were shining as brightly as those of the children.

"It will be a splendid trip, but there's lots to be done before Saturday," she exclaimed. "The girls and I can shop after school tomorrow. Pete and Ricky will need some new clothes, too. I'll go with them on Wednesday afternoon."

The next day, Pam, Holly, and Sue went with their mother to the largest department store in Shoreham. Zip was to have a new collar for the dog show, so he too went shopping. Since dogs were not allowed in the store, Pam fastened his leash to a parking meter near by.

7

In bounded Zip.

The three girls had outgrown their bathing suits, so they stopped at that department first. Holly and Pam were led into a small fitting room to try on new suits while Mrs. Hollister took Sue to the next booth.

The two older girls had each donned a suit when they heard excited yells and running feet outside the fitting room.

"What on earth——" Pam began, when suddenly there was a sharp, happy *woof*, and in bounded Zip with an indignant clerk at his heels.

"Oh, Zip!" Pam cried. "How did you get loose?"

Mrs. Hollister and Sue rushed in. Pam and Holly were laughing and hugging Zip while the saleswoman, who had been joined by the manager, both talked at once.

"Please, please!" Mrs. Hollister cried. "We'll take our dog out at once. And we're very sorry he's caused such a disturbance." Turning to the collie, she said, "Zip, shame on you! Now come with me at once."

Hanging his head and looking very sad, Zip slowly followed Mrs. Hollister out the door. Sue was told to stay in the other booth and look at a magazine.

By the time Mrs. Hollister returned a few minutes later, Pam and Holly had chosen their swim suits. Pam's was a bright yellow and Holly's a red-and-white check.

"Zip is waiting for us outside, and I'm sure he'll stay there now," Mrs. Hollister said, smiling. "While you're dressing, I'll go help Sue try on her suit."

In a few seconds the girls heard their mother calling Sue.

"I guess she didn't stay there." Holly giggled. "Come on, let's hunt for her." They dressed hurriedly and went to join their mother, who had not yet found Sue. Mrs. Hollister hustled toward the elevators while Pam and Holly ran to the other side of the building, where the escalators moved endlessly up and down.

"Oh, dear!" sighed Pam. "I hope the little monkey hasn't tried to ride on this all by herself!"

But Sue was not on it, so the girls turned back.

"Oh, see that crowd!" Pam cried, looking toward the infants' department.

A group of people were standing in a circle, apparently amused by something or someone the girls could not see. Pam and Holly, both struck with the same thought, started toward the spot.

"Do you suppose it could be——" Pam began, and then she saw Sue.

Their baby sister, clothed only in the briefest of bathing suits, was gazing lovingly at a doll that lay in a bassinet on display. She was entirely unaware of being the center of attention from smiling shoppers and saleswomen.

Pam rushed over to her. "Sue," she said, "Mother's looking all over for you!"

"Do you like my new suit?" Sue asked as she was led away. "I was playing Fourda."

In a few minutes the girls found their mother. Amid much giggling Sue's street clothes were put on and the new suit wrapped in a box. When they reached home, Mr. Hollister and the boys chuckled over the story of Sue's adventure.

By Thursday evening suitcases were practically packed and the children could give all their attention to getting Zip ready for the dog show. Pam and Pete washed the collie, and after school on Friday they brushed and brushed his coat until it gleamed.

At four o'clock Zip's young owners proudly led him to the Armory, where the dog show was being held. What excitement there was! Inside the huge brick building people were hurrying in all directions, and the dogs were barking as if impatient for their turns in the show.

Eagerly the Hollisters looked around for the Children's Class section.

"There it is!" Holly cried, and Pete led Zip over to the stall assigned to him.

Right next to their collie, but in another section, was a beautiful white French poodle. On top of its enclosure was pinned a blue ribbon.

"Oh, isn't he precious!" Pam exclaimed as she and the others stopped to admire the poodle before taking seats near by.

Watching class after class of dogs being shown made Ricky restless, so he got up and started on a tour of inspection. When the boy returned to the others, he reported having found a door behind the row of stalls where Zip was located. Ricky had opened it because he wanted to give the dogs some fresh air.

"See how they're all panting?" he said.

"I hope none of the prize dogs run away through that door, Ricky," Pam remarked.

The Hollisters thought Zip's turn to be shown would never come. But finally the Children's Class was announced.

Pam began to feel anxious. Would the collie respond to her directions as well today as he did at home?

Soon she was leading her pet into the ring. How pleased she was to see the collie go through his paces without a moment's hesitation.

"Think we've got a chance to win, Pete?" Ricky asked, tugging at his brother's sleeve.

"I sure hope so," he said. "Pam is a wonderful handler. See how obedient Zip is."

After all the dogs in the Children's Class had been shown, the Hollister boys and Holly sat up straight, almost breathless with suspense. Three judges were walking slowly back and forth in front of Zip and two other dogs.

Finally they wrote on slips of paper, and one of the men carried them to the committee table. The chairman looked at the slips, then picked up the

"Think we've got a chance to win, Pete?"

"Hurray!" cried Ricky. "First prize!"

first-prize blue ribbon. The children felt their hearts pounding as the man began to speak.

"The blue ribbon in the Children's Class, for best all-round dog"—he smiled—"goes to—Miss Pam Hollister for her entry, Zip!"

"Hurray!" cried Ricky, jumping up. "Hurray!"

"We sure have a swell dog!" Pete said.

Just then, Joey Brill, a tall, heavy-set boy of twelve who was always making trouble for the Hollisters, pushed through the crowd and walked over to Zip. Scowling, he said, "You Hollisters think you're the whole show just because your old mutt got a little ribbon!"

"Pay no attention to him, Pete," Pam whispered as her brother made a move toward Joey. "He's jealous 'cause he doesn't have a dog in the show."

Ricky moved in between Joey and Pete and announced firmly that he was taking Zip outside for a breath of air. Holly said she would go along.

Joey now turned his attention to a small terrier who was yipping in a near-by stall. Putting his face close to the excited little dog, the boy barked shrilly while he poked at the animal with his program. Suddenly there was a wild shout from Joey.

"That beast bit me!" he shrieked.

Mr. Brill, who was seated not far away, ran to his son's side. The dog's owner sprang to defend his pet. There were excited words. In the confusion Pam's voice rang out.

"It serves Joey right! He was teasing the terrier!"

The owner repeated the remark to the judges, who had come up to question the meaning of the disturbance. It would, of course, disqualify the terrier if he was proved vicious. Other people who had noticed the incident agreed with Pam, and Joey was asked to leave the Armory at once.

At this point another commotion arose. A Mrs. Milton cried out that her prize-winning French poodle was missing from its stall beside Zip's. The children remembered the lovely animal well. As the crowd surged toward that section of the hall Pam said to Pete, "Do you suppose Joey let him out?"

Before the boy could answer, Holly came racing into the building through the rear door, her pigtails flying.

14

"What's the matter?" Pam asked her as the girl rushed up excitedly.

Words tumbled over each other as she said quickly, "It's a man. He came running out the door Ricky opened. He had Mrs. Milton's white poodle under his arm. Zip's chasing him, and Ricky is, too!"

Before Holly had finished her story, Pete was dashing out of the building with the girls after him. They could see Zip and Ricky going full speed after a man in a bright blue suit. Zip was gaining on him because the dognaper was being slowed down by the struggles of the poodle in his arms.

"Get him, Zip!" Ricky shouted, and the other children took up the cry.

"Get him, Zip!" Ricky shouted.

CHAPTER 2

Zip Disappears

ZIP bounded nearer and nearer to the running man. It looked as though the dog would win the race. But before he could reach the thief, a long black car which had been parked at the side of the road pulled out, and the rear door opened.

The man with the poodle under his arm tumbled in, and the sedan roared down the highway. Zip, baffled for only a moment, tore after it at a terrific clip until he was a mere dot of tan fur in the distance.

"Oh, I wish there were a policeman here to chase that car!" cried Pam, stopping to catch her breath.

"Why, look, there's Officer Cal!" panted Holly, who had turned around to look for one.

The children raced back to speak to the handsome young policeman, who was a friend of theirs.

"I'll go after the thief!" he said, and, striding to his motorcycle at the curb, thundered up the highway.

The door of the Armory had opened to let a stream of people out onto the sidewalk. Among them was the father of Dave Mead, a friend of Pete's. Mr. Mead stopped near the young Hol-

The car whizzed along the highway.

listers and called out, "Hello, Hollisters! Where's that prize-winning dog of yours?"

Quickly Pete told what had happened and said, "Mr. Mead, would you help us follow Officer Cal? He's chasing the thief!"

"Why, sure. My car's right here. Jump in! We'll go after him!" shouted Mr. Mead. "Dave'll be sorry he missed this. He walked home."

The Hollisters climbed in, and the car whizzed along the highway in pursuit of Cal and the man who had taken the prize white poodle. The officer's motorcycle turned off the highway onto a dirt road some two miles ahead, and Mr. Mead followed it.

"This is the old way to the airport," he told the children.

As their car rounded a curve they saw the motorcycle drawn up at the roadside.

"Look!" Pete cried. "That's the dognaper's car in the ditch! I hope they caught him."

Mr. Mead stopped his motor and they all jumped out. There was no one in the black car they had been chasing. Officer Cal was looking it over carefully.

"Where did the thieves go?" Pete asked.

The policeman shrugged. "They disappeared before any of us got here."

"And where's Zip?" Pam inquired.

The officer said he had not seen their pet.

"Let's try calling him," Ricky proposed as the policeman began walking around in search of clues to show where the dognaper and his friend had gone.

"Here, Zip! Zip!" the children called loudly. "Where are you?"

They waited hopefully, but Zip did not come. Ricky beat along the dried shrubbery at the roadside, fearful that their beloved pet might have been hurt and could not answer. The others walked ahead toward a brook that ran under a bridge, looking for some clue to the dog.

Pam was the first to see one. "There's Zip's blue ribbon!" she cried, running down the bank to the edge of the stream. Holly and Pete followed close behind.

From a ragged little bush fluttered a muddied strip of blue silk.

"We'll get the thief," Officer Cal said.

"Officer Cal!" Holly shouted. "Come here, quick, please!"

The policeman hurried over and took the bedraggled ribbon from Pam's hand.

"It's the ribbon Zip won at the show, Officer Cal," cried Ricky, rushing over.

"Then your dog may not be far away," replied the officer.

Several other people had driven up by this time. They ran to the stream, thinking there was a clue to the dognaper. In disappointment a man said, "What about my wife's dog? Her poodle, Champion Fernlake Enchantment, is a trick dog, worth several thousand dollars. You've got to find him, officer!"

Cal nodded and handed the ribbon back to Pam. "We'll get the thief," he said confidently. "There are two counts against him and the driver. The car they were driving isn't theirs."

"You mean they stole it?" Ricky asked.

Cal took a slip of paper out of his breast pocket. On it were three license numbers.

"These are stolen-car numbers," he said. "The second number is the same as the one on the car in the ditch."

Mr. Mead permitted the children to search the near-by fields a little longer, then said he must get home. It was a sad-faced group of children that he delivered to the Hollisters' big house on the shore of Pine Lake.

Mrs. Hollister was as concerned as the children and suggested they put an advertisement in the Shoreham *Eagle* so that it would appear the next morning. The children hurried off to do this. While Pete was writing it out at the counter in the newspaper office, Pam pointed to a sign on the wall that read:

OUR ADS BRING RESULTS.

On the way home from the newspaper office, the Hollisters met Joey Brill. He rushed up and shook his fist in Pam's face.

"I'll fix you for getting me in trouble today at the dog show!" he threatened. "And I'm glad your old dog is missing. Serves you right!"

This was more than Pete could stand. With a

quick thrust of his fist he sent the larger boy reeling.

Joey regained his balance and put up his fists. Then, realizing how angry Pete was and that there were four Hollisters against him, he decided not to fight. With a final jeering remark he slunk away and the children continued toward home.

The Hollister home seemed bleak without Zip racing to greet them in his usual exuberant manner. Mr. Hollister, the children's mother told them, had joined the search as soon as he had heard about the dog's disappearance. They waited hopefully for his return, hardly touching their supper. Their father came back empty-handed.

Mrs. Hollister tried to cheer her family by talking about the Florida trip. But Pam said sadly, "Mother, we just couldn't go away until we find Zip."

Her father looked at the girl admiringly. "I knew you children would feel that way," he said. "I've already canceled our plane reservations. We'll go to Florida only if Zip is found within the next day or two."

At nine o'clock the next morning the telephone rang, and Holly sprang to answer it. A woman's voice said, "Is this the Hollister home?"

"Yes," was Holly's quick reply.

"I think I may have your lost dog," the woman continued. "He limped into my yard yesterday afternoon. But he had no collar on, so I didn't

21

know who owned him until I saw your ad in the morning paper.

"I guess it's your collie," the woman went on, "but I must tell you about the dog. There's something wrong with him. He seems to be badly hurt!"

"Oh, no!" the little girl said fearfully.

Holly turned from the telephone with moist eyes. "That was a Mrs. Parker, a lady who lives at Three Mile Corners. She thinks she's found Zip, but he's hurt!"

"Yikes!" Ricky shouted, bouncing about the room. "Let's hurry out there and see."

Pete offered to call their father and see if he would drive them out to Mrs. Parker's right away. Mr. Hollister, who owned *The Trading Post*, a combination hardware, sports goods, and toy shop

"Someone's found Zip, but he's hurt!"

located in the center of Shoreham, had gone there to check an unexpected order that had to be sent off right away. After this he would be free, as he did not usually work on Saturdays.

"I'll be home in five minutes," he promised his son when Pete told him the news.

"We'll be waiting out front, Dad," Pete said and hung up.

As the four older children hurried into their coats and hats, Mrs. Hollister said, "While you're gone, Sue and I will put a clean blanket in Zip's basket, and we'll have fresh water in his bowl. Oh, I hope he'll be all right!"

When Mr. Hollister pulled into the driveway the children scrambled quickly into the station wagon. He headed for Three Mile Corners.

"Tinker and Indy are tending the store for me," Mr. Hollister said. He referred to a kind elderly man and an Indian named Indy Roades who worked for him at *The Trading Post*.

On the outskirts of Shoreham Ricky suddenly pointed, exclaiming, "Look, Dad! Here comes Officer Cal on his motorcycle."

As the policeman approached, Mr. Hollister honked the horn and stopped. Cal swung his motorcycle around and came alongside the station wagon.

"Any news of Zip?" he asked.

"Yes, we think so," Pam answered. "But we're

"Good! I'll go along as a police escort."

awfully worried about him." She told Cal the story.

"We're on our way to Three Mile Corners now to see if it is Zip," Pete put in.

"Good," said Cal Newberry. "I'll go along as a police escort."

"I'm the President of the United States with my own special police escort," Pete pretended.

Pam pulled herself up regally and said in a haughty tone, "I feel like a queen riding in my royal coach!"

Mr. Hollister chuckled. "I see that Officer Cal has turned off the highway up ahead. Do I have the permission of my distinguished passengers to follow him?"

The children laughed, then said, "Oh, yes, Dad."

"This is the road where the dognapers' car was ditched," Ricky announced. But when they reached the spot, he cried, "It's gone!"

"I guess the police towed it away," Mr. Hollister said.

They went on. The motorcycle began to slow down a few miles farther along, and the Hollisters saw that they were coming to a crossroad where a white steepled church stood bright against the blue sky. As they drew nearer, the Hollisters noticed an attractive yellow cottage nestled among the trees. Behind it a stream tumbled over stones.

"Isn't that the same brook where we found the blue ribbon?" Pete exclaimed. "That's probably how Zip found his way to the Parker house!"

On the lawn of the cottage was a neat sign bearing the name *Parker*. Officer Cal had dismounted and was waiting for them. As they walked together toward the house, a young woman opened the front door.

"You must be the Hollisters," she said warmly. "Please come in. The dog is in the kitchen by the stove."

Would it really be Zip?

CHAPTER 3

An Exciting Plane Ride

"THAT'S our Zip!" cried Pete as he knelt beside the collie who lay on a rag rug near the stove. "Don't try to get up, boy."

The other children crowded around their pet as Zip barked weakly and struggled to rise, his tail wagging feebly. But his left hind leg seemed to be hurt badly and he sank back onto the rug.

"Oh, you poor thing!" Pam petted him sympathetically.

Mr. Hollister stooped to examine the leg.

"That's our Zip!" cried Pete.

"Zip must have been struck by something heavy," he stated. "I don't believe his leg is broken, but he'll probably be lame for a while."

"I'm so glad it's no worse," said Pam. Then turning to Mrs. Parker, she added, "Thank you so much for taking care of him."

"I'm as happy about it as you are," the kind woman replied.

Officer Cal questioned Mrs. Parker about any suspicious-looking people she might have seen in the neighborhood. Mrs. Parker said that she had seen two men sneaking through the field behind the church the afternoon before. One of them was carrying a canvas-wrapped bundle.

"I'll bet the stolen poodle was in it!" cried Ricky.

"You're probably right," the policeman agreed and explained to the woman what Ricky meant.

"I'm sorry to hear that," she said. "It's too bad I didn't notice where the men went."

Pete and his father had already lifted Zip up and were starting for the door. Ricky raced ahead and opened the station wagon. Zip was laid on the rear seat. Pam climbed in and put the dog's head on her lap. Then Mr. Hollister and the others crowded into the front. They said good-by to Officer Cal and waved to Mrs. Parker, calling out, "Thank you! Thank you very much!"

When the Hollisters reached home, Sue raced out and hugged the injured pet. "Oh, Zip," she said,

They carried Zip into the kitchen.

"don't you ever, ever chase a robber man again!"

Mr. Hollister and Pete again lifted Zip up and carried him to the kitchen, putting him down on the clean soft blanket in his basket. His tail beat a happy tattoo.

"He's showing us how pleased he is to be home," Pam said as the children danced about the room.

"I'll call the veterinarian and have him look at Zip," Mr. Hollister said, going to the phone.

A little later Dr. Wesley came and agreed with Mr. Hollister's diagnosis. Zip's injury was not a break in the bone but a severe bruise.

"Someone or something certainly gave him a mean wallop," observed Dr. Wesley. "But you're lucky he wasn't stolen, too. They haven't found a trace of that valuable poodle or of the man who stole him."

Zip seemed much better already, although he was still content to lie upon his blanket most of the time. Knowing he would be all right, Pete said to his father, "How about our Florida trip? Now we can go."

"I'll see if I can get reservations for tomorrow," Mr. Hollister replied.

Then he went downtown, and when he returned home that evening, he said he had good news for his family.

"The reservations are all set. We leave for the land of sunshine tomorrow afternoon."

"In just two more days I'll be swimming!" Ricky cried.

"Be patient, tadpole," his mother laughed. "There's lots to be done here first. For one thing, we must arrange for all our pets to be taken care of."

"I'll bet Indy will keep Zip at his house," Ricky suggested. "Our dog and his are good friends, so Zip won't get lonely."

"I think Indy would be glad to do that," Mr. Hollister agreed. "And I'll ask him to come here to feed our little donkey and the cat and her kittens."

"Maybe Dave Mead would come over every afternoon and exercise Domingo," said Pete. "The donkey needs a good run every day or he'll get lazy."

The boy went off to telephone his friend and found that Dave would be glad to do this. Indy, too, said he would take care of the other pets. The Indian also offered to drive the Hollisters to the airport.

Sunday morning found the whole family up early

to prepare for their trip. After church and a hurried dinner, last-minute items were packed and the suitcases squeezed shut. Indy arrived at the appointed time to take the excited children and their parents to the airport.

"I'll pick Zip up on my way back," the Indian said. "And don't worry, I'll take very good care of him for you."

"Are you going to be a nurse man for him?" Sue asked.

Indy laughed with the others. "Yes, I'll nurse him back to good health while you're away."

When they reached the airport, the five children hurried into the administration building. They felt like old, seasoned travelers, since they had been in planes several times before. After the baggage had

"The Happy Hollisters again! Do you remember me?"

been weighed and tickets secured, the Hollisters went out to wait for the plane.

Soon the great airliner came down on its scheduled stop at Shoreham. The children scampered up the landing steps and into the plane, suddenly stopping short. The pretty dark-haired stewardess laughed and exclaimed, "The Happy Hollisters again! Welcome to Flight 702. Do you remember me?"

"Why, you're Miss Gilpin!" Pam squealed in delight. "I thought you just flew on planes that went out West."

"I was transferred last week," the trim young woman said, "just in time to take you all to Florida!"

The Hollisters sat down, with the three younger children at the windows. Mr. Hollister saw to it that all of them were safely belted in.

The plane motors roared and soon they were speeding down the runway, where they paused to wait for a signal from the tower.

"Here we go!" shouted Holly as they raced across the airstrip.

Soon the plane rose into the air, and the Hollisters removed their seat belts.

"There's Three Mile Corners," cried Holly, her nose pressed against the windowpane. "And I can see the Parker house."

Presently the familiar landscape grew smaller and smaller as the plane gained altitude. Then big billowy clouds began drifting in between the plane and the earth.

"The clouds look like whipped cream sitting in the sky," commented Ricky, pointing.

"I think," said Holly, "they look like little lambs sleeping in pretty blue beds."

Before long there were no "blue beds" to be seen at all between the masses of clouds that had turned gray. The children were glad when, after a while, Miss Gilpin came to sit across the aisle from Pete and Ricky. Pam and Holly were just behind them. They told her about Zip and the missing poodle.

Suddenly Pete had an idea. The dognaper's car was heading for the airport. Maybe he had taken a plane!

"Did you have a passenger last Friday with a white poodle?" he asked. "The man would have been wearing a bright blue suit."

"Did any passenger have a white poodle?"

Miss Gilpin looked startled. In a low voice she said, "Friday evening, just as the plane I was in was about to take off, a man in a bright blue suit rushed up and got aboard at Shoreham. He almost missed the plane."

"Was he carrying a dog?" Ricky asked excitedly.

"No, but he did have a big box with holes cut in the top," the stewardess informed the children. "I wondered at the time if it might contain an animal. The man was a surly fellow, and his hand was bandaged."

"It was!" the Hollisters chorused.

And Ricky said, "I'll bet the poodle bit him."

"Did the man go all the way to Florida?" Pete asked.

"I'm sure he got off the plane at Greenville. That's the midway stop on the way to Florida," Miss Gilpin told them.

"Crickets!" exclaimed Pete. "That's a great clue."

"Where did the bad man sit?" Holly asked.

The stewardess pondered for a moment. Then she pointed to the very seat Ricky was occupying.

"I'm certain it was seat twenty, by the window. And I remember his name, too. It was Fred Smith."

A buzzer rang, and Miss Gilpin went to answer a call from the pilot. Pete wished they were going to stop at Greenville long enough to hunt for the poodle.

"Dad, don't you think we should let Officer Cal know this?" the boy asked.

"You're assuming, of course," Mr. Hollister said, smiling, "that the plane passenger was the thief. We'd better go slow and not accuse anyone unjustly."

Mrs. Hollister laughed. "You children have become such detectives that you think of everything. But I wouldn't count too heavily on finding the stolen poodle."

At that moment there was a whoop from Ricky who had been wriggling around in his seat.

"Look! Maybe this is a clue!" He held up a crumpled piece of paper and waved it in front of Pete.

Pete took the paper and read aloud as he smoothed the page.

"COMING!
THE GREAT WIZARD CIRCUS
SUPERB ACROBATIC ACTS!
ORIENTAL MAGICIANS! TRAPEZE ARTISTS!
AMAZING TIGHT-ROPE PERFORMERS
THE WORLD'S FINEST TRICK DOGS!"

"Trick dogs?" the boy repeated. "That poodle was a trick dog."

"Go on, go on, Pete," Holly urged.

Pete read aloud again:

"SEE WILD ANIMALS AND WILD
MEN FROM THE JUNGLES
ELEPHANTS, LIONS, TIGERS
DON'T MISS THIS WONDERFUL SHOW!"

"Yikes! I'd like to see it," Ricky exclaimed.

"Where's it coming to?" Pam asked.

Pete scanned the paper carefully. "That's funny," he said. "It doesn't say. Isn't that queer, Dad?"

Mr. Hollister glanced at the handbill. "I think it is just a sample setup from a printer, Pete," he said. "That wasn't all he was going to put on it."

Ricky was disappointed and said so. But his father told him he would see plenty of wild animals at the Sunshine Circus where they were going. He advised that the children settle down and read for a while. Sue fell asleep immediately, lulled by the motion of the plane.

Two hours later she awoke and said, "Mommy, the plane feels like a rocking horse. It's awful bumpy."

She was right. The big liner was bouncing up and down like a rubber ball and the clouds now looked more like monstrous waves than gentle lambs. It grew darker and darker by the minute.

The plane dipped and soared again as if it were trying to dodge the oncoming black clouds. Suddenly a torrent of rain pelted against the windows. Miss Gilpin's quiet, reassuring voice was heard.

"The pilot says we should pass through the storm shortly," she informed them. "But if not, we may go down at Greenville and wait for better flying weather."

Pete nudged Ricky. "Crickets, I hope we do. Then we can hunt for the stolen poodle!"

CHAPTER 4

The Detective Club

THE airway grew rougher. Rain bathed the windows with solid sheets of water.

"We're going in for a landing at Greenville," the stewardess announced in a few minutes. "Please double check to make sure your safety belts are fastened. Because of the storm Flight 702 will not resume until tomorrow morning."

"Yikes!" Ricky said to Pete. "That's this plane! We got our wish. Hurray! We can start hunting for the dognaper right away!"

"Please double check your safety belt."

The Hollisters hurried through the torrent.

As the plane glided downward through the wall of dark clouds, the Hollister youngsters enjoyed the tingly feeling of swift descent.

"Daddy, how can the pilot see where we're going in the dark?" Holly called.

"He flies by instruments when he can't see the ground, honey," Mr. Hollister replied. "Instructions are coming to him on his radio from the control tower on the landing field."

His answer gave Ricky an idea for a game. "Pete, you be the man in the tower," he said. "I'm flying in on instruments. Ready. Instructions from the tower, please."

"You must fly around," Pete ordered, "until I tell you the field is clear."

"I'm almost out of gas!" cried Pilot Ricky. "I'll have to bring 'er in right now."

"Look!" Holly exclaimed. "We are coming in! I can see the landing lights! We're nearly on the ground."

In a moment the plane touched down lightly on the runway and taxied up to a large building. When the landing steps were rolled to the plane's door, Miss Gilpin opened it, and everyone got out.

The Hollisters hurried through the torrent of rain to the administration building and shook the water off their clothes.

Immediately Ricky began looking around the big waiting room. He whispered in Pete's ear, "That dog-naper might be in this very room. Let's hunt for him!"

Both boys started off, but were stopped by their father. Calling them back, he said, "Don't wander away, fellows. An airline limousine is ready to take us to a hotel in town."

As they rode through the rain-drenched streets, Sue suddenly piped up, "I'm awful hungry, Mommy. Don't they give out food in this airplane car like they do on the plane?"

Several people laughed, and Mrs. Hollister said, "No, they don't, dear. We'll have supper soon after we reach the hotel."

Before long they stopped in front of a long white building with tall columns supporting the porch roof. The passengers alighted and hurried inside.

As Mr. Hollister signed the guest register the clerk

behind the desk gave the children a friendly wink. "It's not often that we have seven names from one family in our book," he said. "I hope you'll have a nice time here."

"We're going to be pretty busy," Ricky replied as he smiled back. "Do you allow dogs in your hotel, sir?" he added earnestly.

"Oh, yes indeed," said the man proudly. "Did you bring one?"

"No, but we're looking for a dog."

"Well, people often bring their pets here. Why just yesterday—or was it the day before—a man checked in with a white French poodle."

"Oh!" Ricky exclaimed, and the others looked startled.

"We didn't see much of the dog," the clerk went

"Do you allow dogs in your hotel, sir?"

on. "The man kept it in his room most of the time."

"Was it Friday night he came here?" asked Pete quickly.

"I think so. I'll look in the book." He leafed through the register, then turned and said, "Yes. It was Friday, and the man was Mr. Fred Smith from Florida."

The Hollister children gasped. "Did he come by plane?" Pam asked excitedly.

"I'm not sure how he arrived," the clerk answered, puzzled by the youngsters' interest. "When Mr. Smith left, he went off in a private car. That's all I know."

They would have asked more questions, but just then Mr. Hollister told them that the elevator was waiting. "Come along," he said.

Inside the elevator Pete whispered to Pam, "I'll bet Mr. Smith rented a car here."

Pam nodded agreement. "Do you suppose he's going to drive to Florida in it?"

"I'll bet he is. Let's check car renting places in Greenville right away and see what we can find out," Pete suggested.

The elevator came to a halt. The door clanged open, and everyone got out. As the Hollisters followed a bellhop down the corridor, Pete and Pam hurried to their mother's side and told her their idea.

"You see, Mother," said Pete, "if we can only find out where Mr. Smith was going, it'll be easier to trace him."

"Of course I'll go," said Mr. Hollister.

"Yes, dear, of course. You may go to one or two rental agencies after supper as long as they're near the hotel. But Dad must go with you."

As soon as everyone was assigned to his bedroom and hands were washed and hair combed, the Hollisters went down to the hotel dining room.

While waiting for the meal to be served, Pete and Pam made their request to Mr. Hollister.

"Of course I'll go with you," he said.

"Dad, you're sweet!" Pam bubbled.

He laughed. "I'd like to see this mystery solved myself," Mr. Hollister said. "After all, we have a score to settle for Zip. I believe the dognaper is the one who injured him."

By the time supper was over, the rain had ended in what Mrs. Hollister called a Scotch mist. Pete,

Pam, Ricky, and Holly set out with their father. Tired little Sue remained at the hotel with her mother and went to bed very soon.

The first auto rental agency the Hollisters visited had no record of anyone by the name of Fred Smith using one of their cars. And no one with a bandaged hand had come in there Friday evening.

"Sorry I can't help you," the clerk said. "Have you tried the DRIVE YOURSELF agency down the street?"

"No, we haven't," Mr. Hollister said. "Thanks for telling us about it."

They hurried to the place, a large filling station, which also rented cars. Answering Pam's question, a young woman, whose name was Miss Erwin, said, "Yes. We rented a black sedan to a Mr. Fred Smith on Friday night. We certainly regret it, too."

"Why?" the girl asked eagerly.

"Mr. Smith was to have returned the car to our agency this morning," the woman said, frowning. "But we heard nothing until late this afternoon. Then the police down in Georgia reported that our car was found overturned in a ditch."

"That's too bad," said Pam. "I hope Mr. Smith didn't completely wreck the car."

"No, but it will need a lot of repair work."

"Did Mr. Smith have a dog with him?" Ricky asked.

"Yes, he was carrying a white French poodle. Mr.

Smith was in a great hurry to get his pet to a dog show, he said. That's why he wanted the car."

"I'm afraid he wasn't telling the truth," Mr. Hollister asserted. "We think he poodle was stolen. The dog's not ours, but we'd like to see his owner get him back."

"Oh!" Miss Erwin exclaimed, adding how sorry she was that they had rented a car to a thief. "Maybe he was being chased by the police when he abandoned it," she added.

Mr. Hollister nodded. "That could very well be," he said. "The same thing happened in our town."

"Is there anything else I can do to help you people?" the woman asked.

"Perhaps you can," Pam answered. "Did you ever hear of the Wizard Circus?"

"Did Mr. Smith wreck the car?"

"No, I never have," Miss Erwin answered. "But it may have winter quarters in Florida. Lots of circuses do."

"We're going to Florida on the morning plane," Pete put in. "Do you think maybe the dognaper was heading that way?"

"He might be," the woman replied. "Many people travel by car through Georgia on their way to Florida."

"Oh, boy!" Ricky exclaimed. "I bet we find him down there!"

Miss Erwin laughed. "I wouldn't want to be in that thief's shoes with a tribe of sleuths like you children on my trail," she said. "Good luck!"

As the Hollisters walked back to their hotel, Holly looked puzzled. "What did that lady mean about us?" she asked.

Pete answered in a deep, throaty voice. "She means we're the Hollister Super-Sleuth Club, Inc."

They all laughed, then Holly asked, "What does 'Inc.' mean, Dad?"

"That your business firm is a corporation," answered Mr. Hollister. "But I don't believe I'd bother with it for your detective business."

"We'll just call it the H.S.S.C.," said Pete.

"And the first job for the H.S.S.C. is to find that man who hurt Zip!" Pam declared.

"Right!" the others chorused.

CHAPTER 5

Popcorn Troubles

EARLY the next morning Mr. Hollister asked his children, "Is the H.S.S.C. ready to leave?"

They all giggled and said they were eager to continue their detective work. Even Sue declared she was going to find the bad man!

"All aboard, then," their father said, and the young sleuths marched from the hotel and climbed into the airline's big car.

Within half an hour they were aboard the plane once more, and as soon as it was in the air, the children began to tell the pleasant hostess about their evening's adventure.

"I didn't go to the 'gency with them," said Sue, "but I'm a Hollister seus just the same."

Miss Gilpin laughed, and Pete explained about the Hollister Super-Sleuth Club. "Well that's fine," she said. "And now I'd like to serve breakfast to the detectives."

"Please let me help you," Pam requested.

"All right. And how would you like to wear a hostess's cap? I have an extra one."

"Oh, I'd love that," said Pam, and followed Miss Gilpin to the rear of the plane. The young woman set the cap on the girl's head at a jaunty angle. Then

The young sleuths marched from the hotel.

they fixed trays of orange juice, corn flakes, and sweet buns. For the grownups there were cartons of coffee and for the children, milk.

After everyone had been served, Pam took her own seat and started to eat. In a moment Ricky piped up, "Any seconds, Pam?"

"Sh!" Sue called. "That's not p'lite."

"But I'm still hungry," Ricky said. "And besides, she's the other hostess."

Miss Gilpin had heard the boy's request and now came back with a basket filled with all kinds of rolls. She passed it to Ricky, then offered the rolls to other passengers.

"See," said Ricky, leaning forward and poking his sister in the back with his finger, "it pays to ask."

When the children finished eating, they gazed out

the windows. Holly pointed down to a wooded mountain. "It doesn't look any bigger than an ant hill and the roads on it are tiny as pieces of white string."

Mrs. Hollister smiled. "This is the way our world must look to a giant—like the one in *Jack and the Beanstalk*."

Sue's brown eyes grew wide as she asked fearfully, "Are giants *this* tall, Mommy?"

Mrs. Hollister reassured her daughter. "Why, Sue, there are no giants that big except in stories."

"That's good," said Sue, much relieved.

The plane flew on through the sunny sky, and presently Pam exclaimed, "There's the ocean!"

Everybody looked out the windows, and Mrs. Hollister remarked, "What white beaches! We'll enjoy them."

"When can we go digging in the sand?" Sue asked her mother.

"Perhaps late this afternoon," she answered. "We're going to land soon."

Pete asked his father where Circus Island was.

"In a small lagoon near the ocean, about thirty miles from the airport," Mr. Hollister replied. "We'll go there by bus."

In a few minutes the plane began to circle for a landing. Before the Hollisters got out, they said good-by to Miss Gilpin, and Pam murmured in her ear, "Be on the lookout for the man with the bandaged hand. He might be flying North again."

Miss Gilpin promised to be on the alert, and

added, "Good-by and good luck to the Happy Hollisters!"

As the younger children stepped from the plane, they were amazed to find it so warm. The sun was very bright, making them squint.

"Why, it's summer!" Holly said, twirling her pigtails. "And only yesterday it was wintertime in Shoreham!"

"Gee, I wish I could live here the rest of my life," declared Ricky. "Just think, I could swim all year round."

Pam laughed. "But don't forget all the fun you'd miss up North, Rick. No sledding, no skating, no snowballs——"

Ricky wrinkled his freckled nose as he thought

"See, it pays to ask."

about this. "Well, maybe I wouldn't stay here *all* my life," he decided.

When the suitcases were brought from the plane, Mr. Hollister and the boys carried the heavier bags and the girls the lighter ones. The bus stop was only a few feet away.

"Here comes the bus now," Mr. Hollister said. "See, it says Circus Island on the front."

He and Pete put the luggage aboard and then the family climbed in.

"Why, it's practically a private car for the Hollisters," Pam announced, surveying the empty vehicle.

Holly and Ricky ran for seats in the rear. Then suddenly the boy said, "Oh, it's not going to be our own private car after all. Look!"

Two more passengers were climbing aboard. One was a woman and the other a very fat, red-faced man who took a seat directly in front of Ricky and Holly. He at once removed his hat and began to fan himself with it.

The bus started, and for a while the children were quiet. The fat man fell asleep and was soon snoring, which made the other passengers smile.

As they rode along, the young Hollisters stared, fascinated, at the passing scenery.

"Oooh," squealed Holly, pointing to some stately palm trees, their broad fronds waving gently to and fro. "How do the monkeys ever get to the top of those high trees with no branches to hang on to?"

49

The little girl thought all palm trees had monkeys in them.

Mrs. Hollister smiled. "I guess all the Florida monkeys are in circuses or zoos."

"Monkeys wouldn't like these palms anyway," Ricky spoke up. "There aren't any coconuts on them —just leaves."

Mrs. Hollister said there were a great many kinds of palms. "These lovely tall ones are royal palms," she went on, "and never bear any fruit. Some palms are much smaller and look almost like feathery bushes. They're called palmettos."

Suddenly Sue bounced up in her seat and laughed. "But look at *those* trees with long gray hair," she said. "It's hanging down all over the trees' eyes!"

Mr. Hollister explained that this was the kind of moss which grew on oak trees in the South.

"It's not like our moss up North," he said.

"No," Pam spoke up. "Ours is a soft green carpet that grows on the ground under the trees."

Presently the bus came to a stop, and the driver called out, "Children, here is where you can buy the best popcorn in the whole United States. We'll stop for a ten-minute rest."

"Oh, goody!" said Ricky and was the first one outdoors.

Back a little way from the road was a shop with a popcorn machine in the front window. The white kernels were being tossed about so fast that they looked like giant snowflakes in a storm.

Mr. Hollister gave Pete some money and told him to buy a small box of popcorn for each member of the family. When the boy learned that there were several different kinds, he took orders. Mr. and Mrs. Hollister and Pam and Sue took the plain buttered, salted variety. Pete and Holly decided on big molasses balls. Ricky could not make up his mind until he found some small popcorn balls with an extra large quantity of molasses. Then he said this was his choice.

"Only I want some hot popcorn right out of the machine, with not a thing on it," he said.

As Pete handed it to him, he did not notice the twinkle in the younger boy's eyes. The Hollisters got back into the bus. Ricky went at once to the rear and laid his half-opened bag of the small molasses balls on the rack above him. Then he began to munch on the loose popcorn in his pocket.

Pam politely offered some of hers to the woman passenger, who took a little and thanked the girl for her generosity. The fat man was still asleep and snoring noisily, so Pam did not disturb him.

After the bus started, all the children except Ricky sat contentedly nibbling on the popcorn. The redhead was about to do something mischievous.

Making a popgun of his thumb and third finger he sent a kernel of the corn whizzing toward the back of Pete's head. Instantly the boy put his hand up but felt nothing. A moment later he was whacked again.

It landed, kerplunk, on his bald head.

This time he turned around, but everything looked peaceful in the bus.

The next shot from Ricky's fingers misfired and the big kernel landed *kerplunk* on the bald head of the sleeping fat man. He stirred, grunted, and changed position. Ricky stifled a giggle as an idea crossed his mind. If he should climb up to the baggage rack, he could neatly drop pieces of the popcorn right down on the man's head.

Standing on the rear seat, the boy started to pull himself up. At this moment Mr. Hollister turned around and looked disapprovingly at his son. In his haste to retreat, Ricky hit the bag of molasses popcorn in the rack. It opened and overturned.

The sticky contents pelted down plop, plop, plop on the fat man's head!

"Oh!" exclaimed Ricky.

The man awoke instantly, jumping up and clamping his hands to his head. They, too, became sticky. Some of the gooey popcorn lay on the seat and the rest was rolling on the floor.

Seeing Ricky so close to him, the man cried, "You! You! You did that!" His face grew redder than ever.

"I—I'm sorry," the boy stammered. "It just fell."

"Clean up this mess!" the man ordered as he wiped the molasses off his head and hands with a handkerchief and changed his seat.

"Y-yes, sir," Ricky said and gathered up the dusty popcorn balls. Actually he felt more sorry for himself than he did for the man. Now the boy had no popcorn to eat!

Mr. Hollister came back to speak to his son and suggested that he and Holly sit quietly for the rest of the trip. A moment later, the fidgety redhead saw something out the window which made him forget all about the popcorn.

"Yikes!" he exclaimed. "An orange orchard!"

"It's a grove," Pam corrected, adding, "what a pretty sight!"

As far as the Hollisters could see, on either side of the road, stretched the low-growing citrus trees, their fruit brilliant against the dark green leaves.

The travelers stopped at a little stand to buy big glasses of the fresh juice. As they left the orange grove, the bus driver called to Mr. Hollister.

"Excuse me, sir. I thought I'd tell you, if you

haven't made any reservations yet, I can recommend a fine place to stay right across from Circus Island. It's called the Treasure Cove Motel."

"Thank you. We'll take your advice," Mr. Hollister replied.

Pete went forward to talk to the friendly driver. "Have you ever been to the Sunshine Circus on the Island?" he asked.

The man nodded. "Many times in the past five years. It's been a fine show, but I hear that it's going to break up."

"Why?" Pete asked, startled at the news.

"I don't know. The performers are leaving one by one. The sword swallower was aboard my bus just the other day on his way to join another circus. He wouldn't say why he was leaving Sunshine. Something queer about it. You folks know anyone there?"

Pete shook his head. "No, but we've heard that Peppo, the clown, wants to sell his houseboat, and Dad has come down to look at it."

The driver whistled in surprise. "Peppo wants to sell his houseboat? Things must be bad. He owns part of Sunshine Circus, you know. Well, here we are at Treasure Cove," he announced, stopping the bus. "Have a nice time, folks."

"We will," the children cried. "Good-by."

Treasure Cove Motel proved to be a very attractive group of pink stucco buildings with cottages, an outdoor dining room, and a large playground for children among some palm trees. All around were beds of tall poinsettias and flowering hibiscus with a border of rocks.

As the family walked up a pebbled path toward the motel, Holly stopped abruptly. "Look over there!" she cried. "Some real coconut trees!"

On a far side of the grounds stood several palms with heavy clusters of the big brown nuts.

"Gee," said Ricky, eying them with longing, "I wish we could get one."

The words were hardly out of his mouth when *kerplunk*—a coconut hurtled down and hit the ground.

"You got your wish in a hurry, Ricky." Holly giggled, as her brother dashed to scoop up the coconut. Coming back, he asked his father, "How can we open this—it's hard as a rock."

All had the same idea and raced to the lagoon.

55

Mr. Hollister smiled, saying that usually a special, very sharp knife was required. "But I think we can make this do," he added, knocking the coconut against a pointed stone in the flower bed.

It punctured a neat hole in the top and each child had a sip of the delicious coconut milk. Then Mr. Hollister cracked the fruit into smaller pieces for each one to nibble on.

In the meantime Mrs. Hollister had selected a cottage large enough for her family. They followed her inside and began to unpack.

As soon as Holly and Sue had hung their clothes in the closet of the room they shared with Pam, the little girls dashed outdoors. They bumped squarely into Ricky. All had the same idea and raced to the lagoon.

"I wonder if this is where we go swimming," said Ricky. "Boy, I'd sure like to jump in. But Mother said we could only look around till she comes out."

They stood still and gazed across the lagoon to Circus Island. Sunshine Circus looked very gay with its red-and-white striped tents. Flags fluttered everywhere, and from the island drifted the sound of rollicking music.

"I wish we could go over to it," Sue said. "Let's stand on that bridge to the island." She pointed to a low, arched causeway, painted white, that crossed the water to the circus grounds.

The three children ran to it and stood at the entrance. They did wish that their parents would hurry.

"I'd love to be in a circus," cried Holly, hopping up and down.

"I'll be a clown," said Ricky, putting on a silly face and loping around, much to Sue's delight. She laughed and clapped her hands.

"Oh, Ricky, you're a good clown!" she squealed. "Only your face isn't painted."

Holly climbed onto the bridge railing, where she balanced carefully for a moment. "I'm a tightrope walker," she announced.

"Ohh-h, Holly!" Sue cried, frightened. "Be careful."

"Look out, Sis," Ricky warned. "You'll get wet if you miss a step."

Holly laughed as she put one foot cautiously ahead of the other in true tightrope-walking style.

"I am the great Floopsy Doopsy," she told them. "I never miss. OHHH-HH——"

The little girl teetered, waving her arms wildly, then there was a tremendous splash.

Holly disappeared from sight!

CHAPTER 6

Crocodile Capture

SUE and Ricky ran to the railing of the bridge from which their sister had fallen.

"Holly!" Sue shrieked, terrified.

Ricky peered anxiously over the edge of the causeway into the lagoon.

Suddenly the water below them bubbled up and Holly's pigtailed head popped to the surface. Her brother and sister were relieved.

The dripping girl shook her head to get the water out of her eyes and started swimming about. Fortunately she had on a shirt and shorts and light shoes, so the weight of the wet clothing did not bother her. She looked up and saw Ricky peering down at her.

"I guess I'm not such a good tightrope walker after all," Holly said.

Teasingly, Ricky said, "Floopsy Doopsy was Flopsy Dopsy. Your tightrope must have jiggled."

"That isn't a rope, Ricky," Sue told him solemnly. "It's a wooden railing."

"It was a pretend rope, and Holly was a pretend tightrope walker," he explained.

Holly swam around in the cool, peaceful water, and called out, "This lagoon is wonderful, Ricky. Don't you wish you were in swimming with me?"

58

"Holly!" Sue shrieked, terrified.

"I sure do," Ricky cried. "Wait for me. I'll go up and put on my trunks." Then, stopping to look about, he continued, "Say, I wonder why there aren't any people in bathing? It looks super."

"I want to swim, too," Sue said, looking a little forlorn. She disliked being left out of anything.

"No, Susie," called Holly. "It's too deep for you. I can't touch bottom."

Ricky started to run to the cottage, then stopped. It didn't seem right for him to leave Holly in the lagoon with only Sue to watch her. As he hesitated he could hear Holly splashing around happily in the water and he almost wished that it had been his good fortune to have tumbled in.

Just then the door of a cottage a little farther down the bank was flung open and a woman rushed out.

She seemed to be waving to someone and Ricky turned to see who might be behind him. There was no one in sight. All at once he realized that she was calling to him.

"Out!" was all he could hear at first. Then her voice came more clearly. "Get that child out of the water! Hurry! Get her out!"

Above the woman's cries, Ricky tried to reassure her. "My sister is a good swimmer," he shouted. "She's all right."

"Holly's having a good time in the water," Sue added.

"No!" gasped the excited woman, who by now had reached them and was running toward the railing. "Little girl, come back! It isn't safe in there!"

"She knows it's deep," Ricky said, puzzled by the concern of the stranger. "Daddy says Holly swims like a fish."

The woman turned and gripped Ricky's arm. "You don't understand. Yesterday a dangerous crocodile escaped from the circus. People think he's in the lagoon!"

Ricky gasped in fear. He raced to the railing and called down to his sister, "Holly! Come in quickly. It's dangerous out there."

Holly only laughed, suspecting another of Ricky's jokes. Instead of obeying his order, she swam on her back farther out into the lagoon. Ricky screamed at the top of his lungs, "Holly, quick! There's a crocodile in that water!"

The little girl caught the fear in his voice and started to swim toward shore, but she did not hurry. It might still be a trick, she thought. Then Holly saw the woman and heard her call, "Swim faster! Swim faster! Hurry, hurry, child!"

Ricky kept watch of the still waters of the lagoon. Could it be that beneath the calm blue surface there might really be a crocodile very close to Holly?

All at once his straining eyes caught sight of a tiny whirlpool out in the middle of the lagoon. The ripples widened rapidly and then up through the center rose the hideous head of an enormous crocodile.

"There he is!" screamed Ricky. "Hurry, Sis! Hurry!"

He picked up a stone and threw it at the creature with all his might. *Plunk!* The missile struck the ugly snout sharply and it disappeared beneath the water.

Sue, at the first alarm, had run as fast as her little legs could carry her to summon her father. Mr. Hollister came at full speed, arriving in time to see the crocodile's head disappear.

Holly had finally realized her danger. She was a good distance from shore and put on all the speed she could. But her father, to make sure she would be safe, caught up a life preserver which hung on the bridge. From it trailed a long rope. He hurled the preserver across the water to his daughter, just as the crocodile's head appeared again.

"Catch this life preserver!" Mr. Hollister called frantically. "Take a good grip and I'll pull you in!"

The little girl had just looked over her shoulder and had seen the terrifying scaly head of the crocodile coming toward her. Thoroughly frightened now she grabbed the bobbing life buoy and held on tightly. Her father pulled her through the water at lightning speed.

With a mighty heave he dragged her ashore.

"Hurray!" shouted Ricky, jumping around.

Mrs. Hollister, with Pam and Pete, had arrived in time to see the rescue. For a moment Holly's mother clung tightly to her wet little daughter, kissing her snub nose in relief.

"Oh, Holly, darling, you must learn to be more careful. What a narrow escape!"

"Crocodile! Get out of the water!"

"I will. I really will," Holly declared, and she meant it. Her heart was still beating at double-quick time from the frightening experience.

The excitement had brought a group of circus workers running across the causeway. Upon hearing that the crocodile was near by, they ran for ropes and spikes to capture it, and four of them set out from the island in a small motor launch.

The Hollisters watched anxiously as the men started their work. Two of them waded into the water and one of the men coaxed the reptile toward shore by swishing a spike back and forth on top of the water.

As the crocodile neared them angrily, the other man lassoed him around the body. The animal fought desperately, but could not get free.

Meanwhile, the men in the launch took the rope attached to the creature's body and prodded him toward the island. When they reached the bank, the crocodile was dragged off to the fenced-in pool where it lived.

"Thank goodness that's over," said the woman who had warned Holly. Turning to the little girl, she smiled. "They should thank you for discovering the whereabouts of the crocodile. No one has dared go in the lagoon to look for him."

Holly had to admit that her good deed was quite by accident and she was glad it was over. Smiling sweetly at the woman, she said, "Thank you for warning me."

The crocodile fought desperately.

"You were brave just the same, Holly," Pam insisted. Then, looking at Sue, she said, "You were wonderful, too. Nobody else thought of giving Dad an S.O.S."

Sue dimpled with joy at her big sister's praise, but a puzzled look came over her face. "I didn't give Daddy anything," she protested.

Pam laughed. "I mean that you gave Daddy the news that Holly was in trouble so he could help her."

Meanwhile Mrs. Hollister was insisting that Holly run up to the cottage and change into dry clothes. "We're all going over to Circus Island," she said.

Ricky went along with Holly to get a funny clown cap he had found on a table in his room when they arrived. He had lost his desire momentarily to go swimming.

When the two children reached the cottage, Ricky found the key where Mrs. Hollister had hidden it under the mat and fitted it into the door lock. As he started to turn it, the youngsters heard someone knocking on the door of the next cottage. They looked across and saw a short, stocky man in a bright blue suit. One of his hands was bandaged!

Excitedly they gazed at him. Could it be the dognaper?

Leaving the key in the door they stepped across the lawn hand in hand for a better look at the man. He heard them and turned, his bold black eyes staring insolently. Now they were sure he was the person who had hurt Zip and stolen the French poodle back in Shoreham.

"Do you come from Shoreham?" Ricky asked bravely.

The ugly face screwed into a frown as the man growled, "Never heard of the place. I'm the dog warden around these parts."

"What are you doing here?" Holly spoke up. Somehow she couldn't believe him.

"Registering all dogs in this motel, naturally. You got any?" His retort was rudely spoken.

The man turned his back on the children as the door of the cottage was opened by a young woman. To Holly's and Ricky's surprise they noticed that

65

"Do you come from Shoreham?"

under each arm she held a small white French poodle. The man walked in and the door closed, leaving two very puzzled children outside.

"He's the thief. I just know he is," Holly declared in a whisper.

"You bet he is!" Ricky agreed. "Holly, we've got to trap him before he gets away."

CHAPTER 7

A Chase

"HOLLY, I'll watch for the dognaper while you change your clothes," Ricky offered. "When he comes out, let's follow him and see what we can find out."

His sister was not sure they should try this alone. She suggested that Ricky get Mr. Hollister.

"Maybe I should," he agreed and raced off as Holly hurried into the cottage.

While dressing, Holly could see from her window that the suspected man had not come from the cottage next door. Maybe he was the dog warden after all, Holly began to think, even if he did look like the thief and had a bandaged hand.

"Oh, dear, I hope we can find out!" she sighed.

The little girl dashed outdoors to watch for the reappearance of the suspect. She was just in time to meet Ricky and Pete, who explained that Mr. Hollister had gone off to look for Peppo, the clown.

"Pete's going to help us instead," Ricky announced.

The three children went to continue the watch for the man. Pete asked his brother and sister if they were very sure he was the one they had seen running from the dog show in Shoreham.

"I'm positive," Ricky declared. "He ran right past me when he came out of the Armory with the poodle."

"Well," said Pete, "if you're wrong and he *is* the dog warden here, he'll have a badge or something to prove it."

At this moment the door of the cottage opened. Out came the man in the bright blue suit. He ignored the children, striding off toward the street.

"Excuse me, sir," called Pete, hurrying after him. "Please wait. We'd like to ask you something."

The stranger turned with a look of impatience. "Well?"

"This is the dog warden."

"My brother and sister said you told them you're the local dog warden. May I see your badge, please?"

The man turned very red and snarled, "You're a fresh kid. What right have you got to ask that?"

He started to walk off but Pete blocked his path. "We're just interested," Pete pretended. "We've never seen a real dog warden before. Please show it to us."

The unpleasant suspect glared angrily at the Hollisters, then whipped a paper from his pocket.

The boy read the sheet, looked sheepish and handed it back. Putting the paper in his pocket, the man said, "There! Now are you satisfied?"

"I'm very sorry, sir," Pete answered. Turning to Holly and Ricky he announced, "This is Mr. Frank Shaw and he *is* the dog warden."

Mr. Shaw said huffily, "That's my name, all right, and yours ought to be Snooper. Now get out of my way. I'm in a hurry."

With that, he strode to a car and drove off. Ricky stood staring after him. "I don't care if he has a paper to prove he's a dog warden. I know he's the Shoreham dognaper!"

He felt bad to think the thief had gotten away so easily. Nothing Pete and Holly said could persuade him that he might be wrong about the man.

"We'll get him someday. Wait and see," Ricky prophesied as he ran into the Hollister cottage to get the clown cap.

When he returned, the three children hurried off to where Pam, Sue, and their mother were waiting to make the trip to Circus Island.

Mr. Hollister had not returned, so the family strolled along the waterfront toward an inlet that ran at right angles to the lagoon and out to the ocean.

"Don't the boats look pretty?" said Pam, admiring several sailboats that lay at anchor, their tall masts pointing skyward.

"Yes, they certainly do," Mrs. Hollister agreed. "And I like the houseboats. They're so gay and cozy-looking."

"I'd like to live in that one with the candy top," said Sue. She pointed toward Circus Island where three houseboats were moored. One had a red and white striped roof that looked like a peppermint stick.

"Do you suppose one of those boats is Peppo's?" Pam asked.

A boy who was loitering near by said, "Yeah, the one at the far end."

As Mrs. Hollister and Sue started back for the causeway, the others paused to talk to the boy. He was about Pete's age, had green-blue eyes and black hair that stuck straight up on his head. He said his name was Hook Murtine.

"How do you all know Peppo?" he asked with a scowl.

Pete explained why the Hollisters had come to

"I'd like that one with the candy top," said Sue.

Florida, and Holly added, "I can hardly wait to meet Peppo. I just love clowns."

"You all won't like this one."

"Why not?"

"He's mean and so are his kids."

"How do you know?" Ricky asked. He didn't like to think of a clown being mean.

The boy gestured toward the circus and replied sullenly, "I work over there sometimes when they're down here in winter quarters."

"What do you do at the circus?" Pete asked.

"Help Mike, the monkey man," Hook replied. "I carry heavy pails of water for his old animals."

The children listened intently as he continued. "What do you kids do? Or are you rich and just spend Papa's money?" he asked with a sneer.

Before Pete had a chance to say that every one of the Hollister children had chores to do at home and that they often helped at their father's store besides, Hook burst out, "I don't like kids that don't work!"

With that he yanked the clown cap from Ricky's head and started running up the shore with it toward the causeway. As if this weren't enough, he gave little Sue a push as he passed her.

"He can't get away with that!" Pete cried and raced off after the bully, with Pam, Holly, and Ricky at his heels.

Hook was a fast runner, but so were the Hollisters. By the time they reached the bridge, Pete had almost caught up to the mean fellow.

"Get him!" Ricky shouted.

The Hollisters expected Hook to run across the causeway and wondered if they should follow. But to their surprise the bully turned away from it and sped up the lawn of the Treasure Cove Motel.

As he dodged in and out among the cottages, Pete and his brother and sisters kept after Hook. Twice they were almost close enough to grab him but he darted out of the way. The boy must have felt, though, that he was about to be caught, for suddenly he cried out, "Here, take your old clown cap!"

With a swing of his arm he threw it directly into Ricky's face. Then Hook leaped for the street and jumped aboard a bus that was just leaving. From inside he waved tauntingly at them.

"Another Joey Brill!" said Pete in disgust.

"Do you suppose he'll bother us when we go to the circus?" Holly asked.

The children turned and started back for the causeway. Just as they passed the cottage next to the Hollisters, the young woman who lived there rushed out excitedly. Seeing the children she cried, "My precious doggies! I'm afraid they've been stolen!"

She hurried toward the Hollisters, who had stopped short and stood listening in amazement.

"Oh, please *do* something!" she pleaded. "Help me find my little pets!"

He yanked away the clown cap and started running.

CHAPTER 8

An Angry Elephant

"We'll help you find your poodles," said Pam kindly to the excited young woman. But the girl wondered, if they had been stolen, just how the Hollisters would do this. "Are you sure someone took your dogs?" she asked.

The woman, whose name was Mrs. Blake, said that after the dog warden had left she had tied the white poodles in back of the cottage as she often did.

"They never tried to run away," she said, "so I'm terribly afraid they've been stolen."

Ricky looked at his brother and sister. "There! That proves I was right. The man was the Shoreham dognaper and he took the poodles!"

"What do you mean?" Mrs. Blake asked.

Ricky told the story, and Pam added, "We know how you feel, Mrs. Blake. We lost our collie not long ago. But we found him. I hope you'll find your dogs soon."

"They are such wonderful pets," the woman said, almost in tears. "Besides, they're prize winners! Fifi has taken the blue ribbon twice for best of breed in shows and Mimi can do any number of tricks. Oh, what shall I do?"

"We'll help you find your poodles," said Pam.

Pete offered to get in touch with the police, and Mrs. Blake said, "Oh, would you? The phone's right inside the door." The boy dashed into the cottage.

While he was calling headquarters in the town, the woman asked the other children numerous questions. She was particularly interested in hearing that they thought the man who had called on her was not really a dog warden.

"We think he wrote the paper himself," Holly told her.

"You know what?" said Ricky. "The poodle he stole in Shoreham was a trick dog, and Mimi can do tricks. Maybe that's what the man steals —trick dogs!"

Pam looked at her brother admiringly. "Rick, that's a wonderful clue."

"I'll tell it to the police when they get here," Ricky said proudly. When Pete came out, he asked if the officers would arrive soon.

"A policeman will be here in ten minutes," Pete replied.

While waiting for him, the children went on a hunt for clues to the dognaper. In the back yard Ricky found a man's wide footprints and Pete a Baked Rite dog biscuit. Mrs. Blake said her poodles never ate this brand, so a stranger must have dropped the biscuit after coaxing the dogs to him with it.

"You're grand detectives," she complimented the children.

"We're the H.S.S.C.," Ricky told her and explained the meaning of the initials. "Oh, here comes the policeman," he announced.

The officer stopped his car and walked up to the cottage. "I understood your two dogs have been stolen, madam?" he said.

"I think so," Mrs. Blake answered. "I can't find them anywhere. Officer, tell me, do you have a dog warden in this township?"

The policeman pushed back his cap and said slowly, "N-no. Not at the moment. Why?"

"I believe these children can answer your question better than I can," the woman said.

As the officer listened in amazement, the four

young members of the H.S.S.C. told all they suspected about the man who had come to the Blake cottage.

"He has two names," said Pete. "Fred Smith and Frank Shaw."

The policeman nodded. "He probably uses a new one every place he goes. We'll send out an alarm for him right away."

Ricky ran to get the handbill of the Wizard Circus which he had found in the plane. The officer said he had never heard of that particular circus.

"But it doesn't mean there isn't one with that name," he added. "There are lots of circuses in Florida. And this may be a good way to trace the thief."

He thanked the children for their help and then went off in his car.

The next moment Mr. and Mrs. Hollister and Sue walked up, asking what had delayed the youngsters. It was too late now to go over to the island until after lunch. Pam introduced her parents to Mrs. Blake, then Holly said, "The H.S.S.C. has been practicing."

Upon hearing the story, Mr. and Mrs. Hollister were amazed at this latest turn of events and said they were glad their children had been of service to Mrs. Blake.

"Let's hope the police catch up with that man

soon," Mr. Hollister remarked. "He seems to be doing a thriving business."

The family ate lunch in the attractive outdoor dining room and at two o'clock set off for Circus Island. It was a long walk across the causeway, and the Hollisters stopped several times to admire the landscape.

Looking toward the inlet, they saw white sails standing out against the sapphire blue of the sky. Ahead was the emerald green grass and white sand of the island.

"What a picture!" exclaimed Mrs. Hollister.

Sue sniffed the clear, fragrant air and said, "Mommy, it smells like your bestest perfume."

When they reached the end of the bridge, the Hollisters found a high wooden gate barring their

"A man's wide footprint!"

path. A man who was on guard asked why they had come.

"I'm here to see Peppo, the clown," Mr. Hollister told him. "He's expecting me."

The man stepped into the tiny guard house, picked up a phone, and after dialing, spoke a few words into the receiver. Hanging up, he returned to the Hollisters and said, smiling, "Come in."

He opened the gate and pointed to the largest of several red-and-white striped circus tents some distance ahead.

"You'll find Peppo in there," the guard said. "He's probably rehearsing."

The Hollisters thanked him and hurried across the open space. Walking into the tent, they noticed several men at work raking sawdust over the earthen floor.

To one side a tall clown was putting a large black French poodle through some tricks. The animal had a white paper ruff around its neck.

"What a gorgeous dog!" said Pam.

Peppo saw the visitors approaching and stopped the act. The clown was wearing a funny pointed hat. His costume was pure white with big red pompons in a row running up the front. On his feet were extra-large red shoes which flopped as he walked to greet the Hollisters.

The clown's snow white face had bright red dots on the cheeks and a funny round nose made of red putty. He wore a continual grin which

Peppo was putting a poodle through his tricks.

made the children giggle. They knew that the grin was only painted on, but they were sure he was nice, even though Hook Murtine said he was mean.

"You are Mr. Hollister of Shoreham," said the clown. "Right?"

"Right," affirmed Mr. Hollister, and introduced his family. "Don't let us interrupt you," he insisted. "We're in no hurry."

"Then my dog and I will give you a little show," Peppo offered. "Josey and I dress up every afternoon and rehearse. She works better if I'm in costume."

Peppo snapped his fingers at the black poodle who was greeting the visitors with polite wags of her pomponed tail.

"Here, Josey!" the clown said, explaining that her real name was Josephine.

The smart animal trotted over and obediently climbed a gaily painted ladder. Reaching the top, Josey balanced on her two front feet, her unusually clipped back legs high in the air. Then Peppo tossed a ball which she caught in her mouth. With a shake of her head she tossed it back to her master.

The Hollisters clapped with enthusiasm. Josey came down the ladder, made a great leap, and burst through a hoop of rose-colored paper which Peppo held high above her. The visitors applauded again.

"She's the keenest trick dog I've ever seen," Pete remarked in wonder. "I couldn't leap through a hoop that easy."

"I bet I could," Ricky boasted.

Peppo looked over at the boy and motioned for him to come forward.

"Try it," he invited. "Josey will be glad to rest a moment."

Ricky had spoken up quickly. Now he was embarrassed, but his brother dared the boy to make the leap. Ricky walked over and stood beside Peppo.

"Take your time," the clown advised. "Look at the hoop carefully and gauge the distance. Then start from back there and make a running jump." Peppo's eyes twinkled as he held the hoop aloft.

After pacing backward about five feet, Ricky looked steadily at the torn paper hoop. He measured the height with his eyes. Then with a few running steps and a mighty spring, he flew through the air.

Crash! Legs, arms and rose-colored strips of paper all went down together into the sawdust.

"Oh!" cried Sue. "Ricky spill-ded!"

Ricky was not hurt, but he would not try the stunt again. As Josey came up to lick his hand in sympathy, Peppo said, "I guess this is a trick just for four-footed creatures."

Ricky rubbed his shoulder ruefully and grinned. "Josey made it look too easy," he said. "She's a wonderful dog."

Peppo leaned down to pet her. With a note of

Ricky flew through the air.

sadness in his voice—which sounded odd coming from behind the painted smile—he said, "Yes, Josey is a fine dog, but not so good as when she had a partner. Since Nappy left, my act isn't worth much."

"Who is Nappy?" Holly inquired.

"Napoleon," the clown replied. "Josephine's partner. He disappeared mysteriously."

"You mean he was stolen?" Pam asked.

Peppo shrugged. "Who knows?"

Pete whispered in Pam's ear, "Do you suppose Nappy was stolen by the dognaper?"

"Maybe," his sister said softly. "But let's not tell Peppo yet. He seems so sad. When the police find the thief, we can see if he has Nappy, too."

"Right!"

Josey made several more jumps through the hoop. Peppo held it higher each time, but she did not miss once.

"I wish she was mine," Holly said. "Couldn't we have fun with her?"

"We sure could," said Ricky. "Maybe we can borrow Josey sometime."

Peppo spoke up just then. "Would you like to see my houseboat now while I take off my costume and make-up? I can give you directions."

Mr. Hollister said they would rather wait and have him show it to them.

"Very good," the clown said pleasantly. "There are chairs outside my dressing room where you

Josey jumped through the hoop.

can sit and enjoy the scenes backstage in our circus."

They followed him among the tents. On the way they met a man with balloons. He wore a floppy-brimmed hat over his wavy black hair, and the children were fascinated by his bushy, handlebar mustache. Peppo stopped and asked for a large red balloon.

"Thank you, Greco," Peppo said to the balloon man. "This is for a lovely little girl." With a deep bow he presented it to Sue.

"Oh, thank you," she squealed.

Sue was enchanted with the balloon. She strutted along beside the others, giving her new toy the full length of its string.

The Hollisters and Peppo said good-by to Greco

and continued on their way. Outside the clown's tent were benches and several chairs. Parents and children sat down to wait for Peppo. But in a few moments Holly sprang up.

"I'm a trapeze performer," she giggled, holding her arms over her head and swaying back and forth.

"Don't be Flopsy Dopsy again," Ricky warned her.

"Ugh!" Holly winced at the remembrance.

Presently Peppo appeared in the doorway of his tent, dressed in street clothes, and all the paint on his face was gone. The Hollisters were startled to see how very sad his expression was. He gazed about and asked, "Where is my lovely little balloon girl?"

The angry elephant headed for Sue.

85

Sue had been standing beside her father's chair a moment before but had apparently slipped away unnoticed.

"There she is," Pete said, pointing to where the red balloon was bobbing down the aisle between the tents.

Sue was strolling along, stopping to peer into the opened flaps of some of the tents. Mrs. Hollister spoke in a low voice to Pam, "Run and bring her back, dear. I don't think Sue should walk around here alone."

As Pam set off to do as her mother asked, Peppo remarked, "Sue's pretty close to the elephants down there. She shouldn't get too near them in case they're being exercised."

No sooner were the words spoken than a group of elephants suddenly appeared around the corner of a tent. A tall, heavy-set man was prodding and striking at the lead animal, but the trainer seemed to have no control over it.

Pam was running now, with Mr. Hollister close behind. Sue, with no idea of the danger, stood still, waving her balloon. The elephant man did not see her.

All at once Sue's red balloon caught the eye of the lead elephant. He reared, trumpeting angrily, and headed for the little girl.

"Oh!" Pam shrieked. "He'll step on Sue!"

CHAPTER 9

Trapeze Antics

ALL the Hollisters and Peppo were running at top speed now to save Sue from being stepped on by the elephant. They could not possibly reach her in time, though.

Suddenly the clown caught hold of a long rope which dangled from the top of one of the tents. His feet left the ground and he swung up and over the heads of the others, landing directly in front of the elephant.

The beast, startled, stopped his mad dash. Peppo scooped Sue up in his arms and jumped to the side.

"Oh, thank goodness!" the other Hollisters cried, still running.

Now for the first time the elephant trainer realized what had happened. Holding his unruly beast, he glared at Sue and the balloon which was still tightly clutched in her chubby hand. His face became red with rage.

"What are you doing here?" he demanded. "You have no business in the circus grounds!" He shook his fist at the little child.

Sue hid her face on the clown's shoulder as Peppo spoke severely to the man. "You know the

87

rule, Toto. Your elephants must be chained together when you take them out. Besides, you
didn't look ahead of you and clear the way."

Toto scowled and waved his arms. "Why did
that kid have to come here out of visitors' hours
to scare my elephants?" he demanded. "What
kind of a place is this, anyway?"

Peppo's voice was very stern as he answered
the angry man. "Toto, your elephants must get
used to red balloons and children if they are to be
in my circus. They behave badly because you
abuse them."

As the visitors listened in embarrassment, Mr.
Hollister stepped forward. "I'm sorry my little girl
caused such a disturbance," he said. "And we're
mighty grateful to you, Peppo, for saving her."

Ricky took hold of the clown's hand and asked
where he had learned to swing on a rope so well.

"Oh, I used to be a trapeze performer in my
young days," Peppo replied. "But now I leave that
to my little boy and girl."

"Can we see them?" Holly begged.

"Yes. As soon as you've looked at our houseboat
home."

Peppo led the way down to the shore of the island. Mr. Hollister walked beside him with the
rest close behind.

"I own half of Sunshine Circus," Peppo confided. "For five years business was very good. But
we've had a run of bad luck lately. A year ago Toto

88

and his elephants joined us. It seems to me that things began to go wrong after that.

"All my best performers have been leaving," Peppo went on. "They won't say where they're going or why, but I think someone is offering them more money. That's why I must sell my houseboat —to get cash to pay my performers' higher salaries."

As they approached the dock where the houseboat was moored, the Hollisters exclaimed how attractive it looked.

Comfortable wicker chairs stood about under the awning roof. The interior was even prettier than the outside. Flowered curtains hung at the windows of the living room, and bright-cushioned seats lined the walls. Mrs. Hollister praised the taste with which Peppo had furnished his home.

"Peppo," said Mr. Hollister, "it certainly seems unfair that you should have to part with this lovely home. I'm here to buy it for a customer. But isn't there some way you can keep it?"

The clown shook his head sadly. "I don't see any other way to get the money I need to save Sunshine Circus," he said.

The two men began to talk prices, so Mrs. Hollister suggested that the children run outside and play on the shore.

"Why don't you go and introduce yourselves to my children?" Peppo suggested. "They're practicing their circus act around that bend in the shore."

The five youngsters hurried off and in a few minutes came to a little playground where two children were practicing on trapezes. The girl, who had beautiful curly red hair and freckles, climbed down and came over to the visitors.

"My name's Rita," she said. "You must be the Hollisters Daddy said were coming."

"Yes, we are," Pam replied, introducing her brothers and sisters. She judged Rita to be ten years old like herself.

Kit walked up, smiled, and said Hello. He was a slender, serious-looking boy a little taller than Pete. He was thirteen and had brown eyes, dark hair, and very white teeth.

"This is my brother," Rita said. "And Kit, these are the Hollisters."

After the children from Shoreham introduced themselves one by one, Rita chuckled and said, "Ricky, you and I ought to have a freckle-counting contest to see which of us has the most!"

The little boy laughed and then asked if it would be all right to play on the bars.

"Oh, sure. Come on," Kit invited.

"This is lots of fun," Holly called to Pete. "Why don't you try one of the other bars?"

"I will in a minute. But I'd like to watch Rita and Kit. Will you show us the act you do in the circus?" he asked them.

"My name's Rita," she said.

"Sure," the young performers answered together.

Ricky and Holly got down. Kit mounted the platform to one of the smaller trapezes while Rita settled herself on the bar of another near by.

Then they started to swing, back and forth, to and fro. In a moment they slid backwards off the bars, holding on by their knees. On a forward swing, Rita caught the bar of a motionless trapeze, pulling herself onto it. When her bar swung back, Kit made a spectacular leap and caught it with his hands.

Brother and sister pumped hard and soon were swinging to and from each other again. Then Kit twined his ankles in the trapeze ropes and hung head down, still whizzing through the air.

With a quick flip, he caught the ropes with his

hands and came back to a sitting position on the bar.

Now Rita took her turn for a solo. Slipping off the trapeze, she caught it with her strong little hands, kicked her feet forward and went over and over the bar in smooth somersaults.

For their final act, both children stopped swinging, stood on their hands on the trapezes, then suddenly let go! As the Hollisters gasped, Kit and Rita dropped straight down and caught the bars with their feet!

When the performance was finished, the visitors applauded wildly. When Rita jumped down, Pam clasped the girl in her arms crying, "You were wonderful! Kit was, too!"

Pete whistled admiringly and said, "Crickets! How do you do it? I've always wanted to try stunts on a trapeze. About all I can do is swing by my knees."

"Want to try one now?" Kit asked. "I'll show you how to do it."

"Why not?" Pete answered.

"It's all a matter of timing," Kit said as they walked toward the trapezes. "Rhythm is most important."

They climbed onto the junior swings, and Kit showed his pupil how to gauge the time and position of a leap. Pete managed the first one very well and did another alone.

"Yikes!" Ricky cried.

Pete now mounted a higher trapeze.

"I'm not sure that you should try that high one," Kit warned him.

"Oh, I'll be all right," Pete declared. He felt as though he could do anything at the moment.

Peppo and the children's parents came up just as Pete was judging the distance to the next trapeze. Mr. and Mrs. Hollister had no idea what he intended to do, but Peppo on a hunch moved nearer to the sawdust square beneath the boy.

Pete swung higher. Then with a flying leap he sprang to catch the other bar. Everybody gasped.

Pete had missed it by an inch!

As he fell, Peppo alertly broke the lad's fall. Boy and clown went down together onto the saw-

Kit made a spectacular leap.

dust, but Peppo had saved Pete from a serious injury.

Mr. Hollister was there at once to shake the man's hand, and Mrs. Hollister exclaimed, "How can we ever thank you, Peppo? Twice today your quick wit and action have saved our children!"

Peppo laughed lightly and assured them that he was glad to have done it. He turned to Pete and spoke quietly.

"All acrobats begin their training by long practice on low wires, or trapezes, my boy. You were not ready for the advanced work."

"Yes, I know," Pete admitted, crestfallen.

Mr. Hollister said they must leave now, but Rita and Kit asked if they couldn't stay a little longer and play in the houseboat.

"Couldn't we have a tea party?" Sue spoke up.

"That's a fine idea," Peppo said. "Rita, run ahead and put the kettle on." After she left, the clown said, "Rita is our little mother since my wife died two years ago."

The Hollisters expressed their sympathy. Pam felt very sorry for the clown. He certainly was having a lot of trouble. She wished she might help him.

"Maybe there *is* something I can do," Pam thought. "Help him find his missing trick poodle!"

Catching up to Peppo, she asked if he would describe Nappy to her in case she should see the dog anywhere.

Peppo broke the lad's fall.

"Is there any mark on Nappy that makes him look different from other poodles?"

"No, Pam, there isn't," Peppo replied. "But you could never forget his face. I'll get a picture of him to show you."

When they reached the houseboat, he brought out a large photograph of the dog.

"Oh, he's handsome!" Pam declared. "And what a pretty collar!"

"Nappy's wearing his circus finery," Peppo explained. "The elaborate leather collar is covered with imitation jewels of different colors. The dog's collar is purple. It's very attractive against his white hair."

"Then if I see a lovely white poodle with a purple leather collar, I'll know it's your dog," said

Pam. "And even if the collar's gone, I still think I could recognize Nappy's face anywhere."

"Yes," Peppo replied, "and I hope you do find him. It's a great blow to me to have lost Nappy."

"Perhaps he only wandered off the island and will come back," Mrs. Hollister said, trying to cheer up the clown.

"But I can't see how he got out of the gate at the causeway," Peppo replied. "There's always someone there during the day, and at night he was tied in his kennel."

Holly, who had been sitting beside Rita on a window seat, looked up. In a very decided voice she said, "I don't think he left by himself, Mommy. I just know Nappy was stolen! The dognaper took him!"

Rita and Kit looked at her in amazement. "Really?" Rita said. "Why, that's just what Miss Sally thinks, too."

CHAPTER 10

Pete Sets a Trap

"Who is Miss Sally?" the Hollister children asked in unison.

Rita jumped from the window seat and took her father's hand. "Dad, they don't know Miss Sally," she said. "Can't Kit and I take them over to see her now?"

Peppo laughed. "Yes, you must meet Miss Sally. We think she's a pretty wonderful old lady." Then he said to Rita, "I'm afraid it is too late today. You

Rita returned with fancy cookies for everyone.

know Miss Sally doesn't like visitors after five o'clock."

"We'll go another time," Rita promised.

"Tell us about this lady," Pam begged.

"Miss Sally," said Rita, "has a little house on the other side of Circus Island. She was here long before the circus came."

Peppo smiled. "Yes, long, long before. I know that the old lady is very wise indeed and I often go to her for advice."

Kit said he had asked Miss Sally where she thought Nappy had gone and she had replied, "No sensible dog would leave this island of his own free will. He was stolen!"

Just then the tea kettle began to sing, and Rita hurried to the houseboat's galley to prepare the little party. In a few minutes she returned with fancy cookies for everyone. There was milk for the children and steaming hot tea for the grownups.

As they ate, Rita told them Miss Sally made lovely little figures out of sea shells.

"You'll love them," she said.

Sue jumped up and clapped her hands. "Oh, I can't wait," she exclaimed. "When can we go, please?"

All the children looked toward their father, wondering what he had decided about the houseboat and how long they would remain in Florida. He smiled, saying they would spend the rest of the children's vacation at Circus Island.

"Peppo and I are going to talk again about his sell-ing his home. Maybe he can arrange things so he won't have to. In the meantime he wants me to look at some other houseboats, too," Mr. Hollister said.

Peppo nodded and stroked Sue's shining brown curls. "How would you children like to spend tomorrow on Circus Island?" he asked.

"Yikes!" said Ricky. "Lunch and everything?"

"Yes. Real circus fare at our cafeteria."

"Oh, that'll be fun. Thank you," said Holly.

When the girls finished eating, Rita said she would like them to see her bedroom. The four hurried along a tiny companionway to the small stateroom she occupied. It had gay yellow curtains at the windows and a bunk built into the wall.

"Miss Sally made these curtains," Rita said. "And the rag rugs on the floor. She—she's kind of like a mother to me and does lots of things for us."

Across one side of the cabin were shelves of toy animals. Sue began oh-ing and ah-ing over them— pandas, teddy bears of all sizes, and dogs of many breeds. There were also striped red-and-yellow cats, green cows, and purple-printed donkeys standing side by side with kangaroos and spotted leopards.

Among the wonderful array was a wire-haired fox terrier, life-size and very realistic. Sue clasped it in her arms and sat down on the floor.

"Where did you get these 'dorable things?" she asked.

"From people who sell them at the circus in the summertime," Rita replied. "How would you like to take the little wire-haired terrier home with you?"

"Oh, Rita," cried Pam, "you shouldn't."

"I want to," answered the circus child. "Sue will enjoy it lots more than I do. I never play with it any more."

"Oh, thank you, Rita!" Sue cried, hugging first her and then the stuffed dog.

"It certainly looks real," said Holly. "Let's play a joke with it."

"How?" said Sue.

"We'll call Ricky. Watch!" Holly answered, her eyes twinkling.

Going to the door, she called her brother, who came hurrying down the companionway. Holly waited inside the room until he was almost there, then she shoved the play wire-hair out at his feet.

"Oh!" cried Ricky, jumping back. "I nearly stepped on this little do——"

The girls' gales of laughter interrupted him. As they popped out the doorway, he stooped to pick up the lifelike puppy, amazement on his face. Then he grinned.

"Wow! This dog is almost realer than a real one!" the boy declared.

"Rita gave him to me," Sue told her brother joyously as they followed him back to the cabin.

"Look at the time, John," Mrs. Hollister was saying. "We must leave at once. It's five-fifteen. Thank you so much, Peppo, for a delightful afternoon."

"We'll see you tomorrow," Pete called as the family started for the gangplank.

Upon reaching the motel, the boy said he was going over to the Blakes to find out if there was any word of the missing poodles. Pam went with him.

"No," said the dogs' owner when they questioned her. "There's not a trace of Mimi and Fifi. The police found out where the Wizard Circus is, but none of the stolen dogs were there as far as they could tell, although they had no right to search the grounds to make sure."

"And we thought it was such a good clue," Pete sighed.

As the children left the Blake house, they noticed a car drive up to the cottage which was on the other side of the Hollisters'. The manager and another man stepped out and went inside. Then an elderly woman alighted and began to exercise a wire-haired terrier on the lawn.

"Pete!" Pam cried. "He looks just like the toy one Rita gave Sue!"

"He sure does."

Sue came out of the motel just then. The little girl was still carrying the stuffed animal. Seeing the real dog like it, she squealed with glee.

"Look!" she pointed. "That must be my doggie's brother!"

The woman heard her and came toward the group with her terrier.

Ricky jumped back.

"What a clever imitation!" she said, admiring Sue's toy.

Her husband walked from the cottage just then, telling the manager he would rent it. His wife called to him.

"Dan, isn't this amazing? A real dog and a stuffed one that look just alike."

Her husband took Sue's dog in his hands to examine it more closely. "By Jingo!" he exclaimed. "It's the image of Bing!"

All this time Bing had been barking and jumping about, trying to grab the stuffed animal, but they kept it out of his reach.

"Bing's a trick dog," the woman said. She held up her finger and said, "Show the children how you can somersault!"

The wire-hair leaped into the air and neatly flipped over. Then he barked three times when his mistress said, "How much are one and one and one?"

The children laughed merrily, but Pete suddenly became serious as a sobering thought came to him.

"Mr.—er——"

"Easton's my name," the man told him.

"Mr. Easton," Pete said, "are you planning to stay at the motel overnight?"

"Yes, and for several days."

"Then," Pete warned him, "you'd better keep close watch of Bing. There seems to be a dognaper around. He steals trick dogs."

"Goodness, Dan!" exclaimed Mrs. Easton. "Do you remember that odd-looking man who wanted to buy Bing?"

"The one who had the two white French poodles in his car?" Mr. Easton asked his wife.

"Yes," she replied. "Remember, we had quite a conversation with him. You don't think——"

"Was he kind of heavy and wearing a bright blue suit?" Pam asked.

"And was his hand bandaged?" Pete said excitedly.

"Why, yes, as a matter of fact," Mr. Easton answered.

Pete nodded. "That's the man. Where did you meet him?"

"At a gas station in a little town about five miles from here," Mrs. Easton replied.

The wire-haired leaped into the air.

"Does he know where you're staying tonight?"
Pete asked.

Mr. Easton laughed grimly. "He certainly does.
He told us about Treasure Cove Motel. Well, thank
you for the tip, son. I won't let Bing out of my sight."

Pete was glad to hear this, but still he continued
to worry about the whole thing. That evening, after
the younger children were in bed and his parents had
gone over to call on the Blakes, he sat outside thinking.

"Penny for your thoughts," said a voice, and Pam
joined him. "Oh, isn't it nice out here?"

Pam shut her eyes tightly and chanted:

> "Star light, star bright,
>   First star I've seen tonight

I wish I may, I wish I might
Have the wish I wish tonight.

"Now," she said, turning to Pete, "what are you wishing?"

"That I'll catch the dognaper tonight. Pam, I have an idea! It may be crazy, but its worth trying. Has Sue gone to sleep yet?"

"Sue?" Pam asked. "What has she got to do with the dog thief?"

"I want to borrow the toy dog Rita gave her. I'm going to use it to trap the dognaper!"

Pam stared at Pete in puzzlement. "I don't understand. How can you do that?"

"I think the man may come here tonight to try stealing the wire-hair. I'll bet he hides somewhere on the grounds until he sees Bing come outside for his night airing. Then he'll grab him."

"Oh, I see!" Pam exclaimed. "You want to use Sue's dog as bait. Let's ask her for it."

They ran to the cottage and found Sue still awake. When Pete asked her if he might borrow the toy terrier, she took it from under the sheet and gave it to him.

Pete thanked her and he and Pam left the room.

"There's some heavy string around that box of games we brought with us," Pete said. "I'll get it and tie it on the dog."

Pete found the string and tied it securely about the toy dog's neck. Then he carried it outside.

"Look!" he said in a hoarse whisper.

"We'd better watch from inside," Pam advised him.

"Okay. Let's set the dog where the light over the front door will shine on it a little. We can hold the end of the string inside the window of Mother and Dad's room.

"If the man does come," Pete instructed his sister, "I'll try to grab him, and you scream for help."

"Okay."

The hands of the tiny clock beside Mrs. Hollister's bed pointed to nine-thirty when Pete's hand suddenly gripped Pam's arm.

"Look!" he said in a hoarse whisper.

A shadowy figure crouched over and came stealthily across the lawn toward the little dog!

106

CHAPTER 11

Five-Star Circus

PETE jerked the string attached to the toy dog, and the white blur bounced realistically.

"*Yap! Yap!*" Pete tried to bark like an excited terrier.

Nearer to the wire-hair came the shadowy, heavy-set figure. Pete and Pam could now see it was a man carrying a large net. A hat was pulled low over his forehead, shielding his face from the children's view. With one quick motion he hurled the net over the stuffed animal.

Pete was out of the front door before the fellow could snatch up his prey. Pam followed, yelling at the top of her lungs.

"Dad! Mr. Easton! Help!"

With a great leap Pete landed upon the stocky thief, knocking him off balance. They struggled for a second as doors flew open, but Pete was no match for the muscular man. He gave the boy a hard push that sent him sprawling, then raced across the lawn toward the street. Jumping into a waiting car, the fellow was off like a rocket.

Mr. Hollister and Mr. Easton dashed out, hoping

to catch him. But by this time the man had too good a head start.

Pete was crestfallen a moment, then he said, "Anyway I got a clue!" He held up a tiny piece of white cotton cloth with a zigzag blue stripe in it. "This is part of the front of his shirt," Pete told the two men.

"We'd better turn it over to the police," Mr. Hollister suggested. "It may help them trace the man. By the way, was his hand bandaged?"

"I didn't notice," said Pete.

Mr. Easton offered to take the piece of cloth to headquarters. "And Pete, I can't thank you enough for warning me about letting Bing out alone."

Pete handed him the bit of cloth. Then Mr. Hollister said, "It's time for you detectives to be in bed," and the Hollisters went into their cottage.

The next morning Ricky and Holly listened wide-eyed to the story of the previous night's experience, and Sue hugged her beloved toy dog. She did not quite understand everything, but knew that in some way the little animal had been a real hero. After breakfast she carried it over to the Eastons' cottage to see its "brother." The live wire-haired terrier did several of his tricks, and the little girl giggled.

"Come, Sue," Mrs. Hollister called. "The other children are ready for their trip to Circus Island. You want to go, don't you?"

Sue's dark curls flew straight out behind her as she rushed back to their cottage. It would never do to be left behind!

The five Hollisters said good-by to their parents and hurried across the causeway to Circus Island. Peppo met them at the gate. They were surprised to see that he was wearing his white silk clown costume. A wide red grin was painted on his face.

"Good morning, Hollisters," he called, waving a big bright-yellow hoop.

"Hi, Peppo!" they replied.

"Are you going to do p'forming for us?" Sue said.

Holly cried eagerly, "Are we going to Miss Sally's now?"

"Where are Kit and Rita?" Pete asked.

"Hold on, there!" Peppo exclaimed, laughing. "One at a time. First, Kit and Rita are in school."

"You mean even circus children have to go to *school*?" Ricky said in amazement.

It would never do to be left behind.

"Of course," Peppo replied. "We have special tutors for all the children in the circus. Kit and Rita thought you might like to play circus yourselves until classes are over. Then you can all go to Miss Sally's together.

"We have some costumes for you to use," the clown said. "And yes, Sue, I'll perform for you." He smiled at the little girl. "But first I thought you all might like to meet Joni, the baby poodle."

The Hollisters followed Peppo to a fenced-in plot.

"This pup is the daughter of Josey and Nappy," Peppo explained. "She's already learned a few tricks."

He whistled softly, and a little jet black ball of fur came bounding out of the kennel door.

Next the clown led the way to the tent where costumes were kept, and soon all five children were scrambling into bright circus clothes. Pete and Ricky put on tumblers' tights. Pam found a lovely bareback rider's costume, and Holly a trapeze artist's suit. And Sue was zipped into a little white clown costume just like Peppo's!

"All I need is an elephant," Pam declared, twirling excitedly in her bareback rider's dress. "A small one that doesn't get mad," she added, smiling.

"And you shall have it," Peppo promised. "We'll get Timmy on the way to the ring. He doesn't belong to Toto's herd."

"You mean we're going to have a ring all our own?" Pete asked.

"You'll see," Peppo said smiling.

He left the tent and headed for the animals' quarters. The five Hollisters skipped behind him, with Sue clutching the baby poodle.

"And this is Timmy," Peppo said, walking to a very small gray elephant. "He's a friendly fellow, Pam, and you can ride him safely."

Timmy followed Peppo and the children to a large sawdust-filled ring near the causeway.

"Now for that trick I'll show you, Sue," the clown said.

He gave two sharp whistles. In a moment Josey bounded into the ring and leaped gracefully through her master's hoop. Peppo handed Sue a small hoop, and the little girl held it in front of the baby poodle.

"Now, Joni," she said seriously. "You do just like your mommy did."

Joni yipped and stood up on her hind legs.

But Joni cocked her tiny black head to one side, bounced about the ring several times, and refused to jump.

Joni yipped and stood up on her little hind legs. But Sue would not give up, and finally she was rewarded. The pup leaped through the hoop!

The older children had success with their acts more quickly than Sue. With Peppo's help, Pete and Ricky soon had mastered several tumbling stunts, and Ricky could stand erect on his brother's shoulders.

Pam taught Timmy to hold her in his curled trunk while he lumbered around the ring. And Holly had rigged a tightrope between a post and the causeway gate. By the time school was over and Rita and Kit came to the ring, Holly was able to take six steps along the rope without falling.

Peppo smiled and said a circus was not all fun. It was lots of hard work.

"Now we'd better have lunch," Peppo said. "Suppose you children take off your costumes, and I will, too." He turned to his lovely black poodle. "Take Joni back to the kennel with you," he directed.

The two dogs went off, the little one running like mad to keep up with her long-legged mother. The others were about to leave when suddenly Sue screamed.

A huge white bird had swooped down upon them with a loud beating of wings. It darted aloft again and then returned like a dive bomber, barely missing Pete.

"We're being attacked!" Ricky shouted.

CHAPTER 12

Miss Sally Entertains

As THE big bird swooped down again, the Hollisters threw themselves flat on the ground. Holly was the first to rise to her knees, her hands still covering her face.

"Has the bad bird gone away?" she asked, peeking between her fingers.

It was nowhere in sight, and there stood Peppo, Kit, and Rita chuckling and holding their sides.

"What's so funny?" Ricky demanded, sitting up with a bewildered look.

"That bird won't hurt you," Kit informed them. "We'd forgotten you haven't met Buzzy."

"That's a good name for him. He buzzed us like a dive bomber," Pete said ruefully as he and the others rose and dusted themselves off.

"That's how he got his name," Kit said. "He does that to have fun with people."

"Buzzy is Miss Sally's pet crane," Rita went on. "She found him when he was a nestling and raised him. He's really very gentle."

"Look, Buzzy's over there," cried Sue, pointing.

The beautiful white bird was watching them from a hummock of grass not far away.

"I think he's laughing at us," Pete said. "What sort of a crane is he? We don't have birds like that on the lake behind our house in Shoreham."

"Miss Sally calls it a whooping crane," Kit answered. "She says he certainly whoops it up early in the morning!"

Peppo and the Hollister children went to remove their costumes, then they walked to the cafeteria. Ricky was fascinated by the chefs in their white caps standing behind steam tables and serving everyone with enormous ladles and spoons. By the time the little boy reached the end of the counter, his plate was heaped high with fried chicken, biscuits, sweet potato, and corn pudding.

"I sure like the food down here," he confided to Pete, whose servings had been just as generous.

The girls did not take so much to eat, and once Rita saw Pam break off part of a roll and toss it under the edge of the tent.

"What did you do that for?" she asked.

Pam giggled. "I saw Buzzy peeking at us," she said.

Rita laughed. "I guess he's waiting to go with us."

When the children started for Miss Sally's, Buzzy kept pace, sometimes strutting along on his stiltlike legs, at other times flying above them. After a long walk they came in sight of a small brown house tucked in a grove of palm trees and flowering shrubs close to the water.

"That's Miss Sally's bungalow," Kit said, pointing.

"It's just like Red Riding Hood's grandmother's

114

"Let's carry those pails of seashells!"

house in our fairy-tale book," cried Sue. "Isn't it
'dorable?"

As she spoke, a slender white-haired woman came
around a curve in the shore line. She walked toward
them from the beach carrying two pails of sea shells
which seemed to be heavy.

"There's Miss Sally!" Rita exclaimed.

"Come on, Ricky," Pete said. "Let's carry those
pails for her."

The two boys raced ahead. Seeing them approach,
the woman stopped, set the pails on the sand, and
brushed a wisp of hair from her eyes. She had a kind
face, and the Hollisters liked her immediately.

"Goodness!" she exclaimed. "So many children.
How nice to see you all!"

"Miss Sally, these are new friends of ours, the

Hollisters," Rita explained, and introduced each child. "Buzzy nearly scared them out of their wits." She laughed.

"Oh, that funny bird of mine!" Miss Sally said as she shook hands with the Hollisters. "Please forgive him."

She clucked at her pet, who was stepping around daintily. "Buzzy," she said, "your bill is so long it makes you look ferocious. You must mind your manners and not scare people like that."

Buzzy hung his head, and Sue giggled. Miss Sally continued, "You see, children, Buzzy thinks of himself as a real person, not a bird. I often wonder if the other birds laugh at him."

"Aren't you afraid he'll fly away?" Holly asked with great concern. "We had a parakeet once who did."

"Oh, no. Whenever Buzzy flies off, he always comes back at feeding time," Miss Sally said. "I give him little treats." She chuckled. "Buzzy often goes to join a colony of wild cranes who live about two miles from here. But he never stays with them long."

Buzzy suddenly strutted away from the group, his head held high.

"Just look at that!" Kit laughed. "He knows we're talking about him—conceited bird!"

Miss Sally nodded. "Come here, Buzzy, and shake hands with the Hollisters," she ordered. "And don't you ever frighten them again!"

The crane turned back, his long legs moving like

a slow-motion picture. He stopped, raised his right foot, and "shook hands" with Sue, Holly, Ricky, Pam, and Pete.

"Now we're all friends!" Miss Sally said, smiling. The boys picked up the pails of shells as she added, "Won't you come and visit my little home?"

"We'd love to," said Pam. "And may we see your sea-shell figures? Rita told us about them."

"Yes indeed," the woman answered and led the way toward her bungalow.

Entering through a rose-framed doorway, the Hollisters stepped into a sunny living room.

"Ohhh, Miss Sally!" Pam exclaimed, her eyes wide with delight. "How I'd love to live here!"

The room was very neat, and the windows over-looking the water glistened like crystal. Soft hand-hooked rugs in lovely colors lay upon the painted floor, and the comfortable furniture was covered in gay chintz patterns.

"I make rugs in my spare moments," Miss Sally told Pam who was admiring them. "And here," she said, winking at Rita, "is my butterfly collection."

Miss Sally pointed to an ebony shelf upon which were more than a hundred exquisitely-colored butter-flies.

"Why, they're not real," Ricky exclaimed. "They're made of shells!"

"You're right," the woman admitted.

"That isn't all," Rita told the Hollisters. "Look over here." She led them to an old sea chest which stood in the corner of the room. "These are Miss Sally's birds."

Poised on the chest as though ready for flight were some fifty birds fashioned from shells.

"Look! There's little Buzzy," Holly cried, pointing to a tiny crane with the same red topknot.

Miss Sally smiled as she showed them various Florida birds she had made of shells.

Ricky pointed to a pink one with extremely long legs. "Is there really a bird like that?" he asked.

"Oh, yes, indeed," the woman replied, her eyes twinkling. "That's a flamingo. They had nearly disappeared from this part of the country, so Florida now has a reservation for their protection."

"How do you ever make these birds?" exclaimed Pam in admiration.

Ricky flapped his "wings."

"It takes patience, my dear," Miss Sally replied, "and imagination, too. You could make them with a little practice."

"I'd love to try," Pam said. "Wouldn't you, Holly?"

But Holly was not in the room. She and Ricky and Sue had wandered outside to find Buzzy. The crane was not in sight.

"He's probably gone off to tell his bird-friends how he scared us," Sue giggled.

"Say, I have an idea!" said Ricky.

"What is it?" Holly questioned.

"Follow me and I'll show you."

Ricky laughed as he searched among the bushes and presently came up with two enormous fan-shaped palm leaves. At this point Pam ran out to see where the others were.

"What are you going to do with those, Rick?" she asked as her brother skipped toward a shed behind Miss Sally's house.

"I'm Buzzy!" Ricky called back over his shoulder. "Watch me!"

The girls moved closer to see what their brother was up to. Ricky held a palm leaf in each hand and stood on the shed roof, flapping his arm "wings" like a great bird.

Realizing what he was about to do, Pam shouted, "Wait, Rick! Don't jump!"

But he paid no attention to her warning. With another flurry of his "wings," Ricky swooped off the roof. There was a loud *thump* as the little boy landed in a heap on the ground.

"Oh!" screamed Sue.

At first the boy lay still, gasping for breath. Pam rushed forward, fearing he might have broken his legs. But slowly Ricky pulled himself up.

"I—I'm all right," he said. "I just scraped my knees. The old wings didn't work!"

At that moment Buzzy flapped his way lazily over the treetops and landed beside the children. He stepped over to inspect Ricky's knee. Then he looked at the crumpled palm leaves lying beside the shed.

"I guess Buzzy thinks I'm off my top," Ricky said, managing a smile. "He looks as if he's laughing at me."

"There is a twinkle in his eye," Pam agreed.

By this time Miss Sally and the others had come outside. She insisted upon Ricky's going into the house and having his knees washed and bandaged. As she and Ricky disappeared through the doorway, Buzzy walked over to Kit and nudged him with his bill.

"Buzzy wants to play a game." Kit laughed. "Watch this."

The boy chose a long, smooth stick lying near by and walked past the bird, swinging the wood like a cane. Buzzy stalked him for a moment and then made a lunge, catching the cane in his beak.

He flew off with a great flutter of his wings. But

presently he came back and dropped the cane almost at Kit's feet.

"That's cute," said Holly. "Make him do it again."

"You try it, Pete," Kit suggested, handing the stick to his friend.

Pete took the cane and twirled it. Once more Buzzy swooped down, snatched the stick, and darted off into the sky. After that each child took a turn, including Ricky, who came out with both knees bandaged. The crane seemed to enjoy the game as much as the children did.

"I wish we could take him to Shoreham and make him do tricks," Holly said.

"He'd probably freeze to death," Pete told his sister.

When Buzzy tired of the game, he headed off over the trees. Pam and Pete went inside the bungalow to talk with Miss Sally. She was packing a few sea-shell souvenirs in a box for the Hollisters to take along.

"Oh, how kind of you," said Pam. "We're having such a wonderful time down here."

"We sure are," Pete added, "but I hope we can solve the mystery of the dognaper before we leave."

"You mean the one who took Nappy?" the old lady asked.

"Yes," Pam replied. "Why do you think the poodle was stolen, Miss Sally?"

"For several reasons. First, Nappy was never a roamer. Second, there was no way for him to leave the grounds without someone seeing him.

She was packing seashell figures.

"Third," the woman continued, "I saw a strange man cruising about the island the day Nappy disappeared. He was acting very suspiciously, and I have a strong feeling he had something to do with it."

"What did the man in the boat look like?" Pete asked excitedly.

The woman was thoughtful a moment, then she said slowly, "He was a stocky fellow with a mean, cruel face. One hand was bandaged."

"Yes, go on!" Pam urged.

"I don't know what else to tell you about him," Miss Sally said. "There was just one other thing—it may not help you much—the man was wearing a white shirt with blue zigzag stripes."

CHAPTER 13

Water Boys

"CRICKETS! A white shirt with blue stripes!" Pete exclaimed. "That's the best clue you could have given us, Miss Sally."

"It is?" the woman said with a questioning look. Pete and Pam quickly told her about the dognaper of the night before.

"Well, I declare!" Miss Sally said. "I think you Hollisters are wonderful to take such an interest in tracking down this man. I do hope you find him!"

"He hurt our dog Zip back in Shoreham," Pam said, telling Miss Sally all that had happened at the dog show and in Greenville. While she was talking, Kit entered the bungalow.

Miss Sally listened intently, and when Pam had finished, the elderly woman clasped her hands and exclaimed, "It will be a smart man who gets away from you Hollisters!"

Pete laughed and then asked Kit to tell them when Nappy's absence had first been noted.

"Early one morning," the circus boy replied. "When Dad went to feed Nappy, he found the kennel empty."

"If somebody stole him," said Rita, "why didn't he take Josey, too?"

"The man probably tried to, but couldn't manage both dogs," said Pete.

Miss Sally smiled. "I'll bet the poodles put up a good fight," she guessed.

Pete snapped his fingers. "Do you know what I'd like to do? Go and ask people in the circus if they saw anybody who looks like the dognaper and dresses the way he did."

"I'll go with you," Kit offered.

And Ricky said, "Me, too."

Pam knew Sue could not take part in this activity, so she suggested that the girls stay with Miss Sally and watch her make sea-shell birds.

"I'll let you try it, too," the woman said kindly and set out glue, a bundle of pipe cleaners, and a great bowl of shells on her broad work table.

"Yikes! Is he a man or a mountain?"

Pete, Ricky, and Kit hurried back toward the circus grounds, eager to question the performers and workmen. Reaching the place, they went first to speak to the acrobats. Inside the Big Top five young Japanese men and a girl were waiting for a ring in which to practice some tumbling stunts. Kit knew them well and introduced the Hollister boys, adding that Pete had a few questions to ask them.

"In the past few days," Pete began, "did you happen to see a stranger around here wearing a white shirt with blue zigzag stripes?"

The leader of the troupe, a slender, smiling man, knew only a little English, but he seemed to understand. "White shirt—blue lines?" he queried, looking down at his own fancy black satin blouse. "Zigzag for dress-up? Go have fine time?" He laughed and the others in his troupe and the boys joined in heartily.

"Have you seen someone dressed like that, Jo-Jo?" Kit asked.

"No, Kit. Sorry," replied the acrobat.

"Thanks anyway," Pete said, and the three boys turned away.

"Let's try Fatso over there," Kit suggested.

Sitting in an enormous chair on the sidelines was the biggest man Pete and Ricky had ever seen.

"Yikes!" said Ricky. "Is he a man or a mountain?"

Kit laughed as they walked toward the circus's fat man.

"Fatso," he said, "these are my friends the Hollister boys. They're looking for a man they think stole

125

Kit asked Greco about the suspect.

Nappy. He was wearing a white shirt with a zigzaggy stripe. Did you see such a person here? Maybe at night?"

The voice that came from the mammoth man was a surprisingly small, squeaky one. "No," he said, "I didn't see him. But then I sleep a good deal of the time, especially all night."

The Hollisters winked at each other. As they hurried out into the warm sunshine, the boys passed a comically dressed man, carrying a basket filled with candy-striped canes and pinwheels in an array of colors. Attached to the edge of the basket were dozens of balloons on long white strings. He was the man from whom Sue had received the red balloon.

"Where you hustlin' to, Master Kit?" the cane man asked.

"Hi, Greco!" Kit said, and then asked about the suspect.

Greco had not seen such a person, but said he hoped the boys would catch the dognaper. The man's eyes lighted up and he handed each of them a cane.

"These might come in handy for you detectives," he said, smiling.

The boys thanked him and hurried next toward the elephant enclosure, swinging the canes. The trainer was trying to line up his giant animals for a rehearsal. He was the same unpleasant man who had yelled at Sue for getting in his way. As Kit spoke to him, he looked as angry as ever.

"Toto, these are my friends the Hollister boys. We're looking for a man who might have stolen Nappy. He was wearing a white shirt with blue stripes. Have you seen him?"

For a second Toto was visibly startled, and his heavy black eyebrows raised high for a second. He stared at the boys through squinted eyes, then turned his broad back rudely upon his visitors.

"Hey, Toto! Did you hear my question?" Kit called.

The man whirled and glared menacingly. His great voice boomed, "Get out of here, kids! I'm too busy to be bothered by nosey youngsters asking questions. Now skat!"

Realizing that the mean fellow would not talk, the boys walked away. But Pete wondered if it was all meanness on Toto's part or whether he knew something he would not tell.

"Let's try Mike over at the monkeys' cages," Kit proposed. "But be careful of the baboon. He's a bad-tempered fellow."

Mike was a scrawny little man with bright eyes. He greeted the boys pleasantly. In reply to Kit's question he answered that he had not seen a stranger in a zigzag blue-striped shirt.

"Sure and they hardly wear shirts at all around here," the monkey tender replied in a rolling Irish brogue. "I'm so busy tryin' to keep these little creatures fed and their cages clean that I don't have time for ganderin'. And, begorrah, today my helper doesn't show up!"

"I'm really working in a circus!"

"Then perhaps we can help you, Mike," Kit offered.

The man's troubled face broke into smiles. "And would ye now?" he asked, greatly pleased. "If ye could just take these buckets and fetch me some water, the three of ye, it would take a powerful lot of trottin' off me pore feet."

The three boys picked up the pails and went off to the hydrants for water.

"Oh, boy," Ricky shouted gleefully, "I'm really working in a circus! Wait 'til I tell the kids back home!"

They were returning with the filled buckets when Pete exclaimed, "There's Hook Murtine—over by the monkey cages. He seems to be mad about something."

"He always is," Kit said.

"Looks like he's arguing with Mike. I'll bet he was the helper that didn't show up," Ricky guessed.

The boy was right, for Mike was scolding Hook as they arrived with the buckets.

"You all could 'a' waited for the water 'til I got here," Hook was saying, " 'stead o' lettin' those guys horn in here." Then Hook turned to Pete and Ricky. "What right you all got bustin' in and takin' other folks' jobs away from 'em?" His eyes were blazing, and his fists were clenched. "Why don't you kids get lost?"

Hook gave the boy a shove.

Pete gazed at the boy calmly. "We don't want your job."

"You're jest atryin' to get me fired!" Hook yelled.

With an ugly leer he put out his foot, at the same time giving Ricky a shove. The smaller boy fell headfirst into one of the large buckets.

As Ricky rose, spluttering, Pete rushed at Hook. Down went the two boys into the sawdust, rolling over and over.

"Hit him, Pete!" Ricky shouted.

The monkey man put his hands on his hips and watched closely. "Sure and it's glad I'll be to see that Murtine lad get a lickin' for once. Pete is a fine broth of a lad, and I'm hopin' he beats the daylights out of the rascal."

It seemed to be an even match as the two boys wrestled on with all their might. Before long a crowd of circus folks had gathered to watch.

"It's a good show," observed the living skeleton to the tattooed man.

One of the trapeze performers spoke to Kit. "Who's the blond kid?" he asked. "Friend of yours?"

Kit answered proudly, "Yes, Jack, a very good friend of mine. Isn't he terrific?"

"If he can knock some of the conceit out of Hook Murtine, he'll be a hero around here." The other laughed.

"Here," a woman aerialist said, coming over to Ricky and handing him a towel. "Dry yourself. Your brother's all right. He can handle this Murtine fellow. Oh, look out there, boys! Don't get too near the baboon's cage!"

The last part of her remark was shouted at the wrestlers, who had rolled closer and closer to the monkey cages. The next instant they banged against the baboon's cage and the door swung open.

Inside, the great creature, who had kept his eyes fixed on the fighting boys, dropped on all four feet. In a second he came snarling through the opened door directly at them!

CHAPTER 14

The Tattooed Juggler

PETE's back was turned toward the baboon as the animal jumped out at the two boys. But Hook saw the beast, let out a scream, and dashed off.

"Run, Pete, run!" Ricky shouted frantically.

As the baboon raised its front paws and opened its mouth, the tattooed man leaped from the crowd and streaked toward the uncaged animal. Reaching down he grabbed the beast's short tail

Hook saw the beast and let out a scream.

Mike forced the beast back into his cage.

and whirled him around, just as the baboon lunged at Pete, teeth bared.

"Look out!" Ricky pleaded.

At this moment Mike rushed forward with a long pole and forced the beast back into his cage.

"Hurry!" cried Ricky.

"Hurray for Flippon and Mike!" The human skeleton applauded.

The onlookers all talked at once, thankful for the narrow escape. They knew the power of the mean baboon.

As Pete shook hands with his rescuers, thanking them, Kit introduced the tattooed man as Flippon, the best juggler in the Sunshine Circus.

"Thank you," said Pete, who was still trembling from the shock. "Thank you both!"

"Sure 'n' it was a pleasure," Mike said modestly. Then he shook his head. "Begorrah, I can't figure out how the baboon's cage got unlocked."

Pete looked at Kit. Could the cage have been unlocked on purpose? Poor Peppo! One thing after another was going wrong for him.

When the excitement died down, Ricky said to the tattooed man, "How did you get all those pictures on you, Flippon?"

"Come over to my tent and I'll tell you all about it," the fellow invited.

The three boys picked up their new canes, which had been dropped during the scuffle, and followed the performer. In front of his tent were several camp chairs.

"Sit down here, boys," he said, stripping off his blue denim shirt.

"Crickets!" Pete cried, gazing at the man in astonishment. "I've never seen so many tattoos!"

Grinning, Flippon threw out his chest. Completely covering it was a great American eagle. The bird's head was tattooed clear up to Flippon's neck and when the juggler swallowed it looked as if the eagle were moving its head.

The boys laughed, and Kit said, "Tell them about the eagle, Flip."

The juggler explained that many years before he had been a sailor. One time while he was in Singapore he had felt very lonesome for the United States.

"So I had a man there tattoo the American eagle on me," he said with a smile.

"It's nifty," Ricky said in admiration.

"Wait 'til you see the picture on his back," Kit remarked.

Flippon turned around quickly. Across his back was tattooed a beautiful blue-and-red lion, standing on its hind legs. The animal's claws were bared as if to strike.

"Gee!" Pete exclaimed. "He sure does look fierce." The boy stared at it closely. "Isn't that the lion England uses as an emblem?"

"Yes," said Flippon. "My mother was English, so I had the British lion tattooed on me in honor of her country."

"Gee!" Pete exclaimed.

"Now show them your trick with the sailboats," Kit said with a chuckle.

"Sailboats?" Ricky asked excitedly.

"Watch them move," the juggler said with a laugh.

He turned to face the boys again and placed the palms of his hands back of his neck. On his biceps were tattooed two pretty schooners in full sail. Flippon wiggled his muscles, and the sails actually looked as though they were being rippled by a heavy wind.

"Yikes!" Ricky cried in astonishment. Then thinking what fun it might be, he asked Flippon about having his arms tattooed.

The man shook his head. "Don't ever do it, son. You know, they never come off. Once put on, they're part of you for the rest of your life, and sometimes you get mighty tired of being all marked up."

He laid a hand on the boy's shoulder. "If you want to play tattoo man, have someone paint pictures on your arms or chest. But be sure they'll wash off easily."

Flippon now took Ricky's cane, spun it in the air, and caught it neatly. "You might try this trick, too," he said, reaching for Pete's and Kit's canes.

Deftly he juggled the three sticks. They twisted and turned in the air as Flippon tossed them like lightning from one hand to the other.

"That's keen!" Pete declared. As he looked up

"Come back with that!" Pete cried.

to watch a particularly high throw, he noticed a big white bird directly overhead.

"Look! There's Buzzy!" he shouted. "I wonder if he's hunting for us."

There was a loud flapping of wings and the crane swooped down.

"Hey, watch out, Flippon!" Kit cried.

But he was too late. Buzzy zoomed low over Flippon's head and neatly grasped one of the canes in mid-air.

"Come back! Come back with that!" Pete cried, but the mischievous bird headed off in the direction of Miss Sally's house.

Laughing, Flippon continued to juggle the two remaining sticks with one hand for a few moments, then tossed them to Pete and Ricky.

As the boys were about to leave, Pete suddenly remembered why he had come to the circus grounds. He said to Flippon, "We're trying to find a man who might have stolen Nappy. He was wearing a white shirt with a zigzag blue stripe. Did you happen to see him around here at the time the dog disappeared?"

"Why no, I didn't," the juggler replied. "And it's a shame. Nappy's a fine performer. Kit's probably told you about the tandem act."

"No, I hadn't," the circus boy answered, and went on to explain how Josey and Nappy rode a double bicycle and did hand stands and other acrobatic tricks on it. "The act was one of our main attractions," Kit said sorrowfully. "That's why Nappy's loss is such a blow to my father."

"It's a shame," Pete declared, more determined than ever to track down the dognaper.

The boys kept on with their sleuthing until every circus employee had been questioned. Not one of them had seen the suspected man.

"He must have sneaked ashore from a boat when everyone on the island was asleep," Kit stated.

The Hollister boys were about to say good-by to their circus friend, when they saw Rita, Pam, Holly, and Sue walking toward them. Upon hearing about the juggler, Sue said, "I want to see him jiggle!"

The others laughed, and Kit said that maybe

the juggler would show her some of his tricks. As they approached his tent, the little girl said, "He is jiggling!"

"He certainly is!" Pete agreed.

The jolly performer was dancing a little jig, at the same time tossing four blue balls high into the air.

"He must have glue on his hands!" Holly giggled as they stood and watched. "He never misses."

Just then Flippon stepped underneath one of the blue balls and let it hit his head. It bounced off and sailed high into the air. Then *ping!* the ball landed squarely on top of Holly's head. Quickly catching the ball, Flippon laughed.

Everything was topsy-turvy.

"Oh, I miss once in a while, just like I did then."

"You did that on purpose!" Rita teased him.

"Well, what can I do for you children now?" Flippon said, balancing a ball on the end of his nose.

Ricky spoke up. "Would you let us look at all the things you use in a real circus performance?"

"Why sure," Flippon replied. "Come into my tent," he invited, throwing back the flap.

Rita and Kit excused themselves, saying they had practicing to do, and left. The Hollisters then followed Flippon inside. Everything in the tent was topsy-turvy. Several open suitcases containing canes, balls, and fancy hats stood on the ground. Two cartons were partly packed with clothes. Off in one corner stood an open brass-bound trunk.

"Say, it looks as if you're moving!" Pete observed.

Flippon raised his eyebrows. "Perhaps I am."

"You mean you're leaving Sunshine Circus, too?" Pam asked a little nervously. The man did not answer. "Goodness," the girl thought, worried. "Is this nice juggler going to desert the circus like some of the other performers have?"

She quickly whispered her fears to her brother Pete. The boy gulped and said, "Flippon, you're not going to leave Peppo's circus, are you?"

Instead of replying, the juggler walked to the door of the tent and looked out across the circus grounds. Sue ran up to him and tugged at his hand.

"Oh, please don't go 'way!" the little girl pleaded. "I want you to stay and bounce balls off my sister's head."

This made the juggler chuckle. He turned and lifted Sue high into the air, spun her around a few times, then sat her down.

As he leaned over, an envelope fell from his pocket and landed on the tent floor. Pam bent over to pick it up. She gasped upon seeing the return address on it.

"Oh!" she cried out, putting her hand to her mouth.

"What's the matter? Did it bite you?" Flippon said.

Pam did not answer.

"What's the matter, Sis?" Pete asked.

"It's—it's the name written in the upper corner," the girl said, pointing.

The children crowded close to her. On the envelope was written *Return to Wizard Circus.*

CHAPTER 15

Lost!

WHEN the Hollister children recovered from their surprise, Pete said to Flippon, "Tell us about the Wizard Circus, please."

At first the tattooed man looked a little flustered. He told them that it was a new circus being organized in another section of Florida.

"The owners are getting together some new acts," he said. "They wrote asking me if I would join their circus."

"Will you?" Pam asked anxiously.

"I might," came the reply. "They've promised to double my salary. Several other Sunshine performers have gone there, so it must be a good outfit. I may go, too."

"Oh, please don't leave Peppo!" Pam burst out.

And Pete exclaimed, "This is such a fine circus!"

The juggler looked down sadly at the children. "I can't tell you any more about it," Flippon replied. "You'll have to ask Toto."

"Toto!" Pete thought. "There's something very strange about this deal!"

He thanked Flippon, and the children left the

juggler's tent. As they went through the circus grounds, Pete suggested they ask Toto about the Wizard outfit.

Pete led his brother and sisters past the elephant enclosure to a big brown tent beyond. The flap was thrown back, and Toto stepped out.

"Don't you kids ever go home?" he barked, scowling.

"Oh, yes, sir," Pete answered politely. "We're on our way to the motel now. We just stopped to ask what you know about the Wizard Circus."

Toto's face reddened until Pam was afraid he would explode. "Get out of here, all of you!" he shouted. "And stop meddling in other people's business."

He looked so threatening that the children backed off. Pete wanted to insist upon an answer, but Pam dragged him away.

"Isn't that man awful!" Holly exclaimed as they hurried toward the causeway.

Sue was clinging tightly to Pam's hand in fear, and the older girl decided she would change the subject.

"What do you suppose we're going to have for supper?" Pam tried to make her voice sound gay.

"I don't much care," Ricky said. "I'm starved. I could eat a whole whale." This made Sue giggle.

It was not whale but red snapper which was served to the Hollisters on the motel dining terrace that evening. During the meal the children

143

told their parents about the day's adventures, and Mrs. Hollister gasped.

"My goodness, you've had a lifetime of adventures in one day," she said.

Mr. Hollister looked very serious. "I don't like the frightening aspects of it," he said. "Please, children, don't go on the circus grounds again unless I'm with you."

After an angel food cake dessert, Sue leaned close to Holly and said, "Shall we give it to Mother now?"

"Yes," Holly said and winked at Pam. The older girl winked back and nodded her head.

"Mother," Holly said sweetly, "we have a surprise for you."

"Really? How nice!" Mrs. Hollister said.

"Okay! Open your eyes, Mother."

"Close your eyes." Sue giggled. "And hold out your hands."

As her mother did this, Pam reached down for a package she had hidden beneath her chair. Raising the box above the table, she placed it carefully in her mother's outstretched hands and cried gleefully, "Okay. Open your eyes, Mother!"

"Gracious, what is this?" Mrs. Hollister exclaimed.

Mr. Hollister and the boys were as mystified as she was. Ricky began to fidget.

"Please hurry," he begged, getting up and going to look over her shoulder.

Finally the paper was off. Mrs. Hollister gasped in delight.

"What a beautiful gift!" she exclaimed. "Birds made of sea shells. Is this some of Miss Sally's work?"

The girls giggled. "No, Mother," said Pam. "We made them—with Miss Sally's help, of course."

"They're perfectly lovely," Mrs. Hollister said. "Thank you very much, girls."

Their father examined the delicate work and shook his head. "I don't see how you ever did this." He held up one large muscular hand. Chuckling he said, "I never could with this!"

The others laughed, and Sue said, "Daddy, your hands were made for *big* work."

As they left the table, Mrs. Hollister thanked

They hunted for pretty shells.

her daughters again and gave each of them a kiss on the cheek. "When we get back home," she said, "I'll put my lovely birds in a group on my desk. They'll be a nice memento of our Florida trip."

Ricky all this time had been wishing he, too, had a gift for his mother. Finally the little boy decided he would get one.

"I know what," he thought. "I'll go to that place down the shore they call Sea Shell Beach."

This was some distance from the motel, but Ricky figured he had plenty of time to get there and back before bedtime. He would hunt and hunt until he found his mother the biggest, prettiest sea shell she had ever seen!

For a moment Ricky hesitated. He knew he

should tell his parents where he was going, but he also wanted to keep his gift a secret.

"I'll ask Holly to come with me," he decided.

His sister was eager to go and said she would keep the secret. The children told Mrs. Hollister they were going for a little walk and promised to stay away from the water.

The two skipped off happily and in about ten minutes reached Sea Shell Beach. How amazing it was! The sand was fine and white. And everywhere there were little shells and big shells of all colors and shapes. At once Holly began to pick them up and in no time the pockets of her shirt and shorts were filled.

But Ricky had not yet saved any he had picked up. The boy had examined many but none was that extra special kind he wanted for his mother.

Then suddenly he spotted it—a large pure pink shell shaped like a cornucopia. It had an amazing number of perfectly matched swirls on it.

"Holly, look!" he exclaimed, holding the shell to his ear to listen for the sound of pounding surf in it. Ricky had once been told that this was the sign of a perfect shell.

Sure enough! The shell he had found was perfect!

"It's beautiful!" said Holly. "Oh, Mother will be——"

The little girl stopped short because out of the corner of her eye she had seen a white poodle galloping up the beach. A man was legging after it as fast as he could.

"Ricky!" Holly cried and her brother looked up.

The dog was heading straight for them, and in a moment they could see his collar plainly. It was a fancy purple one with jewels on it!

"That's Nappy!" Holly cried. "He got loose from the dognaper and he's going home!"

"Go to it, Nappy!" Ricky screamed.

The sight of the children evidently made the dog change his course, for he headed toward a grove of moss-covered trees that lined the shore at this point. As he reached it, Nappy turned once more toward Circus Island.

But he got no farther. To the children's com-

A man dashed out and scooped up Nappy.

plete astonishment a large fish net had landed over Nappy, completely covering him and tumbling the dog over and over. Before he could pick himself up, another man dashed from among the trees and scooped up the dog.

As he disappeared into the grove, Ricky shouted, "He's the Shoreham dognaper! Holly, we mustn't let him steal Nappy again. Come on!"

The boy dashed after them, with Holly at his heels. In his haste the boy dropped his prize shell in the sand, but did not pause to pick it up. The children could just vaguely make out the fleeing figure. Nappy was yelping loudly, but in a moment he stopped. This made Holly and Ricky anxious. Had the dognaper harmed the poodle?

The youngsters found the going difficult. The grove of trees became a swamp as they dashed on and time after time they splashed through mud nearly ankle deep. Twice they had to run around the edge of little ponds which the thief had waded through. He was getting way ahead of them, but the children kept plodding on bravely.

Then suddenly Holly skidded on the marshy ground and fell flat. Ricky stopped running to help her up. She was mud-spattered and breathless.

By the time the children were ready to start on again, the dognaper and Peppo's trick poodle were out of sight. Ricky and Holly went on for a distance, then realized the chase was hopeless.

"Anyway," said Holly, "we'll go back and tell the police. They'll find Nappy."

The children started retracing their steps. They stumbled along over huge twisted tree roots, through mud, and around little ponds. Swamp grass lashed at their ankles. It was growing darker by the second.

After they had walked for nearly fifteen minutes, Holly said, "Rick, are you sure we're going right?"

"No, I'm not," her brother admitted. "It seems awful far back to the beach. Let's try this way."

He turned to the right, with Holly following close behind. By this time the daylight was almost gone, and the youngsters felt it would be dangerous to continue.

"Oh, dear," said Holly, a little fearful, "I think we're lost."

"I guess we are," her brother agreed. "But don't worry, Holly. Florida jungles don't have lions or tigers in them. Nothing's going to hurt us—even if we have to stay all night."

Holly was not quite sure, but she knew she must be brave. "Let's sit down and rest a minute," she suggested. "Maybe Daddy and Mommy will come for us."

The children found a large dry clump of grass and sat down. Almost at once they became drowsy and, stretching out on the ground, soon were fast asleep.

Dawn was breaking when the youngsters were awakened by a shrill chorus of bird calls. For a few seconds they looked around startled. Then realizing they were still in the swamp and that no one had come to find them, Holly said, "Oh, Ricky, we're still lost!"

"That's okay, Holly," he said. "We'll soon find our way out."

The little girl hoped so and trudged after her brother. The swamp, a brilliant mass of colorful flowers, birds, and unusual foliage, stretched endlessly around them in the early morning light. Presently Ricky had to admit it was not so easy as he had thought to find the beach. Nothing looked familiar to him.

The children plodded on bravely.

151

"What'll we do?" Holly said, her lower lip quivering.

As Ricky stood still trying to figure this out, the children heard a squawking sound overhead. Looking up, they were amazed to see a huge white bird circling above them. It flew down and stood before them on its long, thin legs.

"Buzzy!" Ricky exclaimed.

The crane stared at the children. How Holly wished she, too, could fly and follow Buzzy back to Circus Island! "You come along with us on foot," Holly invited and started walking.

But Buzzy did not budge. Instead, he began to *whoop* loudly. As the children turned to see why, the bird stalked up to them, grasped the edge of Holly's shorts in his bill, tugging her toward him.

Ricky laughed. "I think he's trying to tell us something."

"What?"

"That we're going in the wrong direction!"

"Let's follow him then."

They set off in the opposite direction with Buzzy, now quiet, parading just ahead of them. After some distance, Ricky suddenly stopped short and said, "Listen!"

From far away came a faint call. Buzzy flapped his great wings loudly and took off over the heads of the children in the direction of the sound.

Ricky cupped his hands to his mouth and shouted, "Hal-lo-o-o!"

Buzzy flew down.

The children heard a faint answer. Someone was looking for them!

"Hello! Hello!" they cried excitedly.

Soon Buzzy returned and flew just above, guiding them from the air. The lost youngsters hurried on.

Each time they stopped to listen for the "hello," it sounded nearer. Finally, through the trees, they saw a figure, and Miss Sally's voice rang out, "There you are! I knew Buzzy could find you!"

The children rushed up to her. "Oh, Miss Sally, we're so glad to see you!" Holly cried.

"Are you all right?" she asked. As they nodded, she said, "My, what a scare you've given everyone! Folks from the motel, your circus friends, everybody around these parts has been helping your parents hunt for you two all night. Where have you been?"

Holly and Ricky told her what had happened. Then Miss Sally said, "You poor tykes! Come! I'll lead you back to the motel. It's not far now."

They walked a short distance, came to the edge of the woods, and started up the beach.

Suddenly Ricky said, "Please wait just a second while I pick up my shell."

He found it in a minute, then they continued on to the motel. What a joyous reunion it was! Buzzy was given full credit for the rescue, and everyone petted the lovely crane.

Peppo and his children were among the throng that was on hand to greet Holly and Ricky and they thanked the children over and over again for trying to rescue Nappy.

"Since the dog broke away once," Peppo said, "I'm sure he'll try again."

Everyone hoped so, but several of them were secretly afraid Nappy might be gone for good this time.

Mrs. Hollister took Ricky and Holly to the cottage to bathe and change their clothes. The boy gave his mother the lovely shell. She smiled as she kissed him.

"It's the most beautiful shell I've ever seen," she said. "And I shall always treasure it." Ricky was very proud. "But please, dear," Mrs. Hollister

"Oh, we're so glad to see you."

added, "next time you and Holly chase a dog-naper, take Daddy with you!"

They promised they would and started for the motel dining terrace.

As the family was finishing breakfast, Mr. Hollister said he had planned a trip for the day.

"Oh, what is it?" Sue asked, clapping her hands.

Her father chuckled. "Suppose you all guess. I'll give you a hint. It may help solve the mystery and it may help me in my business. In any case, it will be fun."

CHAPTER 16

Through a Glass Floor

THE first one to guess where the trip was to be was Pete. "I think the mystery part in it is that we're going to Wizard Circus," he said.

"Right," Mr. Hollister nodded.

Pam's eyes suddenly lighted up. "I have a guess about the part to help your business, Dad. We're going to look at another houseboat."

Her father laughed. "I can see the Hollister Super-Sleuth Club is working again," he said. "One guess from each of you, and you're right the first time!"

Mrs. Hollister smiled and said no one had to guess about the fun they would have. Any time the Happy Hollisters were together they had fun!

"You're right, Elaine," her husband agreed. "But there is a special treat we'll have on the way. Suppose we keep it a secret."

The children tried to make him tell, but he only laughed. He suggested that everyone get ready to leave as promptly as possible. Then he added, "Pack swim suits and pajamas. We might stay overnight."

By nine o'clock everyone was ready to leave. Mr. Hollister had rented a station wagon in town, just like theirs at home. Mr. Hollister and the family took their usual places; Mrs. Hollister and Sue in front, the girls in the middle seat and the boys in the rear.

Mr. Hollister drove for two hours through open, sandy country sprinkled with groves of grapefruit and lemon trees. How sweet it smelled, they thought!

Presently they came to a canal and Mr. Hollister took the road that ran alongside it past pink, blue, yellow, and green cottages. He stopped in front of a houseboat, and everyone got out. A stiff breeze was blowing, but it was warm.

The houseboat was not so attractive as those at

They started off for Wizard Circus.

Circus Island, and Mr. Hollister decided at once that it would not be suitable for his client.

"I'm not even going inside," he said. "We'll push on as soon as you've all had a chance to stretch your legs a bit."

The children played tag for ten minutes, then got back into the car. Mrs. Hollister, sighing, took a comb from her purse and began to comb Sue's hair.

"The trade winds are wonderful," she said. "It would be dreadfully hot without them, but they're disastrous for hair." Gazing at Pete's blond head, she laughed. "Not a hair out of place in a crew cut. Perhaps we should all have crew cuts, girls."

"Oh, no!" Mr. Hollister exclaimed in horror.

"I like our hair the way it is," Sue announced. "I don't want anyone to cut off my curls."

"All right, Sue," Pam said. "Mother may have a crew cut."

The boy and their father laughed loudly at the thought of the pretty mother going about with a crew cut.

At twelve o'clock Mr. Hollister drew up beside a white concrete building set in a palm grove. Among the trees on one side of the building were gay-colored tables and chairs. Beyond was a lagoon with many small boats on it.

"We'll stop here for a little sightseeing," Mr. Hollister announced, "and then have lunch."

He led the family into the building and down a

The children played tag for ten minutes.

long flight of steps to a circular room where great glass-enclosed tanks lined the walls. Swimming about in them were tropical fish of various kinds.

"Crickets!" Pete said, staring at a small mass of misty waving tentacles. "What's that?"

"The sign by the tank says it's a sea anemone," Pam told him.

A few feet away Sue and Holly were laughing. "See these cowfish with horns," Holly called, pointing to a pair of goggle-eyed fish whose faces looked like those of tiny cows.

Beside them a spotted thick-shelled fish gazed out with great popping brown eyes. Ricky read the sign. "That's a trunk fish," he told his sisters. "But he looks more like a hippopotamus."

More fearsome than most of the others was an

unfriendly giant ray. It moved through the water with great batlike wings, as though it were flying. The fish bumped its flat nose against the glass in an effort to strike at the children.

After the Hollisters had looked at all the fascinating sea creatures, they went upstairs to the outdoor dining room to have lunch.

"Boy!" Ricky said, gazing at the green water of the lagoon. "Now's the time to go swimming. I'm hot!"

His father shook his head, saying, "Not now, Ricky. We must eat. Then after lunch we're going out in a glass-bottom boat."

"What's that, Daddy?" Sue asked.

He explained that these rowboats had heavy glass floors so one could look down through the water and see the plant and animal life.

When lunch was finished, he found an old skipper waiting at the end of the dock with a three-seated rowboat. Everyone piled in. Ricky was the last one aboard and made it with a flying leap. He sat down in the stern beside Pete, wishing he was in the water with the fish. It would be much cooler there.

As the little boat started off, strange, colorful fish could be seen swimming beneath the craft. Mr. Murdoch, the skipper, explained the various underwater marvels. But Ricky was not paying attention. Slowly he was taking off his shirt and shoes.

A moment later, Pete, who had his head very close

to the glass bottom, jumped back. A large object had swum directly under the boat.

Pam began to laugh. On a hunch she had turned around. Ricky was gone!

"It's Ricky!" she said.

"So it is!" Mr. Hollister said, thinking how his mischievous son had arranged for a swim anyway.

"I guess Ricky's the biggest fish in the lagoon," Holly giggled.

"Not quite the biggest," the skipper said. "I'll bet Old Faithful would outweigh him."

"Who's Old Faithful?" Pam asked and they all turned to look at the ruddy-faced man.

"That's what we call the giant green turtle who lives in the lagoon," Mr. Murdoch explained. "He's a Florida glider turtle and he's been making this his

Ricky made it with a flying leap.

home since long before anyone in these parts can remember."

"Where'd Ricky go?" Holly asked, worried. She could not see him anywhere.

Suddenly a spray of water shot into the boat. Everyone turned to glimpse Ricky's dancing eyes, a stream of water spurting from between his front teeth.

"Ricky," said Mrs. Hollister, "I want you to——"

The boy did not hear her for he had made a neat surface dive and disappeared.

"Your boy's a real tadpole," the skipper remarked.

"That's what Mommy calls him," Sue giggled.

Presently Mrs. Hollister became concerned. Why didn't her son come up for air? He had been down for what seemed a very long time.

"Ohhh, I see Ricky," Holly suddenly cried out, pointing through the glass floor.

At the bottom of the lagoon was Ricky, upside down, legs kicking wildly. He seemed very busy at some special task.

"What on earth is the boy doing?" Mrs. Hollister exclaimed.

"Maybe he found a pirate treasure," Holly suggested.

"Or an oyster with a pearl in it," Pete added, winking at his father.

All at once there was a great splashing of water and the boy began to rise. Ricky, his impish face red from lack of air, popped his head above the surface

The boy was upside down, legs kicking wildly.

and called out panting, "Help me, someone. He's awful heavy! But what a prize!"

Ricky was treading water as fast as he could, but the odd-looking object struggling in his arms kept pulling him under. Mr. Murdoch laughed loudly, but it was several seconds before the Hollisters could learn the reason for his mirth.

"He's wrestling with Old Faithful," the skipper said. Leaning over the side, he quickly explained to the boy that the giant turtle must be put back. Old Faithful was a lagoon landmark and pet.

Ricky released his huge prize. Then sorrowfully he scrambled back into the boat.

"Shucks!" he said. "Old Faithful would have been swell to have in Shoreham."

His father laughed. "He'd have made a lot of

turtle soup. As for me, I could do without it. I'd prefer that the turtle stay on the bottom of the lagoon."

"Me, too," said Sue, who had never tasted turtle soup. But she decided if her daddy did not like it, she would not either. She made everyone laugh by adding, "The turtle's so hard, I guess he doesn't have much juice in him anyway."

After gazing down at the fish and plants in the lagoon a while longer, Mrs. Hollister suggested that perhaps it was time to go on.

"You H.S.S.C.s still have the mystery part of this trip to solve," she reminded the children.

"That's right," said Pete. "Are we going to the Wizard Circus now?"

"Yes, Pete."

"How far is it, Dad?"

"Only another ten miles."

Pete asked the skipper if he had ever heard of it.

"Oh, yes," Mr. Murdoch replied. "The folks from Wizard eat here once in a while. I take 'em out to watch the fish sometimes. I guess it's a change from watchin' the circus animals all the time."

"Do you know anything about the man who owns it?" Mr. Hollister questioned.

"Not much, except what the folks tell me. I hear a lot of them left other circuses to go with Wizard, and now they regret it."

"Why?"

"Well, I'm not sure. They're well paid, but they

just don't like the way the owner runs things. I guess he's hard to get along with and——"

As the skipper paused, Pete said, "Yes, please go on."

Mr. Murdoch was thoughtful a few moments as he pulled slowly on the oars. Finally he said, "I'm not one to gossip, but you look like nice folks, so I suppose it won't hurt to tell you what some of the bareback riders said one day. They don't think the circus is being run honest."

The Hollisters gasped. Such a place could be using stolen trick dogs!

By this time the boat had reached the dock, and the visitors scrambled out. They thanked the skipper for the ride and his information about Wizard Circus and said good-by. As they started up the path to the parking space, Pete cried out, "Crickets! Look! Isn't that Toto coming out of the restaurant?" He pointed to a big man hurrying toward a near-by car.

Before the other Hollisters could catch a glimpse of the man's face, he had ducked into the automobile. It started quickly and sped down the road.

"I'll bet he's heading for the Wizard Circus!" Pete said.

"Do you suppose he's left Peppo's circus for good?" Pam exclaimed.

"I hope he has," Sue said. "And all his naughty elephants, too!"

"Let's follow him, Dad!" Pete urged and dashed ahead to open the car door for his mother.

Mr. Hollister was willing, and everyone scrambled into the station wagon. They kept the elephant trainer's car in sight for a couple of miles, then in a little town it disappeared in traffic.

Realizing the children's disappointment, Mrs. Hollister said, "We aren't sure that man is Toto. But if he is and he's heading for Wizard Circus, we'll see him when we get there."

"That's right! Of course we will," Pam said.

It was four o'clock when they came to the village where Wizard Circus was located. Mr. Hollister asked a policeman in the center of town to direct them to the circus grounds. Following his instructions, they drove straight ahead and about a mile out of the village turned onto a gravelly road. It was hot and treeless. There were no houses, just hummocks

Ricky scrambled back into the boat.

of grass in the sandy fields.

Presently Ricky let out a whoop. "There it is! I see it!" he exclaimed.

The boy pointed to a group of brown and yellow canvas tops just visible over a high board fence.

As they drew closer Pam said, "Listen!"

"Boy, are they off-key!" Pete remarked. "They sound like a bunch of real amateurs compared to Peppo's band."

"They sure do! Ouch!" said Ricky, clapping his hands over his ears as a trumpeter hit a wrong note.

There was no parking lot in sight, a fact which Mrs. Hollister remarked seemed strange. Her husband pulled the car off to the side of the road and stopped. They all got out.

Around the circus grounds, set some distance back in a field, was a high board fence crudely built, as if it had been constructed in great haste.

"Isn't there any entrance to this place?" Ricky asked as they walked for some time along the fence.

Holly had pranced ahead and was the first to spy one. "Here's the gate!" she called. "Right up here. There's a big sign on it!"

The others quickened their steps. Reaching the entrance, they found it closed and locked. On it in bright red paint had been printed the words:

Absolutely No Visitors Allowed at Any Time.

CHAPTER 17

A Telltale Collar

A SHOUT of dismay went up from the children as they stared at the No VISITORS sign on the locked gate of Wizard Circus.

Pete gave a low whistle of disgust. "And after we drove all this way, too!" he exclaimed. "Dad, we can't just turn around and leave without finding out if this is where the stolen trick dogs are!"

"No, we can't." Mr. Hollister's voice was firm. "We'll stay in the village overnight. In the morning we'll make it our business to be admitted to the circus grounds."

"Isn't there a knothole we can peek through and see what's going on?" Holly asked hopefully.

The children searched but did not find one, though they circled the entire grounds. Once they saw a low door just big enough for a man to crawl through but it, too, was locked on the inside.

The Hollisters waited for a while to see if anyone entered or left the circus, but no one did. At six o'clock they gave up.

As they walked back to the car, Pete said glumly, "We seem to be getting nowhere fast."

Ricky had an idea. "Why don't we post a guard at the circus to see who goes in?"

Pam, too, had an idea. "How about Pete and I asking for a tryout for a trapeze act? While we're waiting, we can look around."

Mrs. Hollister shook her head. "If you had to go through with it, you might have to take too many chances. You're not expert enough to fool circus people."

It was a disappointed little group that went to bed that evening. But by morning the children were full of enthusiasm again to continue their sleuthing.

Pete, Pam, Ricky, and Holly were up at dawn, long before their parents and Sue. Pete said how about the four of them walking up to the circus grounds to see what was going on. Ricky and the girls liked this plan, and Pam went in to ask her mother's permission.

"All right, dear," Mrs. Hollister said sleepily. "But be sure to stick together. And be back here in an hour for breakfast."

"We will, Mother," the girl promised and hurried off to tell her sister and brothers that they would have to make a quick trip of it.

"I guess all the circuses will be going on tour in a little while," Pam remarked.

Pete said this was all the more reason for solving the mystery of the stolen trick dogs. After the Wizard Circus moved away, it might be difficult to trace.

"Oh, look!" Ricky said suddenly and pointed ahead.

The little detectives ran toward the truck.

The huge gate of the circus grounds had opened. Thinking that they might see something to help their detective work, the children began to run ahead. A truck drove through the opening, turned in the opposite direction, and sped down the road. Before the children could get a peek through the open gate, a guard closed it. The Hollisters reached the spot just in time to hear a bolt slide into place.

"We're sure having bad luck," Pete said. "Well, let's do a little exploring. Maybe we can pick up some kind of clue around the fence. I saw lots of papers and things yesterday."

The children began a systematic search. Ricky found an old pasteboard box, but it was empty. A few minutes later Holly picked up a duplicate of the Wizard Circus handbill which they had found on the plane. After this they walked for several minutes, seeing nothing more important than discarded cartons and pieces of rags.

"It's a regular dump around this circus," Holly remarked presently.

Pete said the whole outfit seemed very shabby to him. "But I'd sure like to get a peek at the inside."

The boy had hardly spoken when Pam gave a little squeal. She had leaned over to pick up a twisted, dust-covered mass of leather. Straightening it out, the girl suddenly realized that it was a dog's collar. The license tag was gone and someone had tried to pry off the plate bearing the owner's name. But it was still visible.

"Pete! Rick! Holly! Come here, quick!" Pam cried excitedly.

As the others rushed over to look at her find, Pam pointed to the name plate on the collar. To the others' complete astonishment she read:

"*Zip, owned by Pam Hollister, Shoreham Road, Shoreham.*"

For a few seconds the children were too stunned to speak. Then Pam said, "The dognaper must be here! He grabbed Zip's new collar and pulled it off when he hurt him!"

The children decided that finding Zip's collar made it necessary for them to act at once. The girls thought they should hurry back and get Mr. Hollister, but Pete and Ricky had another idea.

"I think we ought to climb the fence and find

that dognaper before he runs away!" Ricky declared.

"All right, let's do it," Pam agreed.

Their hearts beating wildly, the children discussed how to get over the fence. At last Pete offered a solution. They would go to the place where they had seen the little low door. Pam and Ricky could boost Pete up and he would drop down on the inside. Then he would unlock the door and let the others in.

The boy climbed to his brother's and sister's shoulders and pulled himself up. Fortunately no one on the other side was looking in the direction of the fence and he dropped down. In a moment the others were inside, too.

As they gazed ahead, wondering which way to go,

He would let the others in.

the Hollisters decided that this was indeed a shabby circus. They could not understand how the owner could afford to pay higher salaries to his performers than Peppo could.

Going forward cautiously, the children approached a rickety circus wagon. Outside of it a washing was strung from the door to a near-by pole. Garments on it flapped limply in the slight morning breeze.

Suddenly Pete grabbed at Pam's arm. "See that shirt on the line!" he whispered.

It was a white shirt with blue zigzag stripes. The center of the shirt had been torn.

"The dognaper's shirt!" Pam said in a low voice. "He *is* here!"

"What'll we do?" Holly asked nervously. "Maybe we'd better go get Daddy now."

"Just a minute!" Pete said. He was looking toward a strange sight in front of a faded brown canvas tent. "See that man!"

The others looked. The fellow was tall and thin and at this moment he was swallowing a shining sword!

"Oh, goodness!" Pam whispered.

Holly was fearful the man would hurt himself, but as they gazed in fascination he withdrew the sword and laid it on the chair in front of the tent.

Pam had been thinking. Now she said, "Even if he is a sword swallower, I think he looks nice.

Maybe he'd tell us about the person who lives in this wagon."

The others agreed and they hurried to speak to him. On the way Pam whispered to Pete, "Maybe he's the sword swallower who came from Peppo's circus—the one the bus driver told us about."

Her brother nodded just as the man turned his head. He smiled at the children.

"Good morning," he said. "You must be the early birds one hears so much about."

Pam introduced the Hollisters and said they were not part of the circus. They were passing through town and had come to look around. The sword swallower lifted his eyebrows, saying he thought no visitors were allowed.

The children looked at one another, but did not explain. Quickly Pete said, "Are you the sword swallower who was with the Sunshine Circus?"

The man nodded glumly.

"We've heard from Rita and Kit how wonderful you are. They say Peppo will never find another sword swallower like you," Pam said.

The man brightened and he remarked briskly, "Of course not." After a moment he said, "Peppo is a fine fellow. How is he doing?"

"Poor Peppo," Pam said sadly. "He is not doing well at all. His best performers are leaving Sunshine."

"I am sorry already that I left Peppo," the sword swallower said.

They went forward cautiously.

As he started to go inside his tent, Pete asked, "Can you tell us who lives in that wagon over there where the wash is on the line?"

"Certainly," came the reply. "Professor Mars lives there. He's a great dog trainer—so he says. He has an act with trick poodles which I have not yet had the pleasure of seeing." He went inside.

The children could hardly contain themselves. As each wondered what their next move should be, the door of Professor Mars's wagon opened. A man came out and stood on the top step. He was looking the other way, so he was unable to see the Hollisters.

"He's the dognaper!" Ricky whispered excitedly.

As the children shrank out of sight behind a packing case to watch him, the professor ran down the steps of his wagon and across the grass to a small enclosure surrounded by a high wire fence. A sound of frenzied barking commenced. At once the children followed it.

Opening the gate in the fence with a key, the man went in and unlocked the door of a large dog house. Inside were four snow white French poodles. They retreated to growl and bark at their keeper.

"They're the stolen poodles!" Pam said tensely.

"And see how badly he treats them," Pete exclaimed with wrath. "He's hitting them with that rope."

Pam started from their hiding place, determined to save the dogs from further cruelty, but her brother held her back.

"If we give ourselves away, we'll never catch him," Pete warned. "We'd better run now and get Dad to bring the police."

The children backed up and, trying not to be noticed, hurried along past the various tents and wagons. They reached the fence out of breath.

Pete unlocked the door and first Holly, then Pam scrambled through and started running down the road. As Ricky was about to follow, a heavy hand was laid on his shoulder. Another grabbed Pete by the arm.

"No you don't," said a cruel voice as both boys were yanked backward and the door locked. "You Hollister kids have bothered me for the last time!"

Professor Mars!

He was holding Pete while another man was grasping Ricky. As the boys opened their mouths to yell for help, the men's hands were clapped over them.

"One word out of you two and you'll be sorry!" the dognaper said. "Get moving to my wagon!"

Ricky was quivering with fear and tears started to form in his eyes. When Pete saw this, he put an arm around his brother's shoulders.

"That's all right, Rick," he whispered. "We'll get out of here some way. Come on. We'd better do as they say for now."

The brothers marched on ahead, with the two men stalking along behind them.

CHAPTER 18

A Special Performance

PRODDED every few seconds, Pete and Ricky were taken to Professor Mars's wagon and made to sit on a low bunk. The man who had been holding Ricky glared at the professor.

"You sure got us in a fine jam," he said. "What are we going to do now?"

"There's only one thing to do, Nero. Scram out of here fast."

"You're right! Let's start packing."

Pete and Ricky looked at each other. What if the men should escape before Mr. Hollister could come with the police?

The older boy was determined to find out what he could in case the men should get away. Looking at the professor, he said, "There's no use trying to run off, Mr. Fred Smith."

Nero spun around. "Fred Smith? Why you know——"

"We know all about you," Ricky said. "You stole Champion Fernlake Enchantment from the Shoreham dog show. And you hurt our Zip when he chased you. You're going to get punished for being so mean."

178

"We'll lock these kids in here!"

The men laughed harshly. "We won't be caught!" said Professor Mars, who was stuffing shirts into an old suitcase. "We'll lock these kids in here, Nero, and get out fast."

The boys' hearts thumped wildly. If they could only stop these dognapers!

Pete went on, "You went snooping around Sunshine Circus and stole Nappy. And later when you found out there were a couple of other trick poodles at our motel you took them too—Mimi and Fifi, I mean."

Professor Mars was very nervous. "Yes, yes, we did all that," he admitted. "We needed dogs for our act and we didn't have time to train new ones."

"But Nappy got away for a while," Ricky said.

"Yeah, that dog was smart. He got out of our car

near Sea Shell Beach and almost found his way to Circus Island. But we caught him again."

By this time the two men had finished packing their bags. Mars pointed a finger at the two boys and warned, "Now stay where you are! We're going to lock this door from the outside. Not a word out of you for at least half an hour!"

The two men stepped out of the wagon. But before they had a chance to lock the door Pete said, "Come on, Rick!"

The boys flung themselves at the door. *Crash!* It swung open, knocking both men to the ground.

"Why didn't you tie those kids up?" Nero shouted, jumping up.

"I'll do it now!" Mars answered.

But before he had time to rise, Pete was astride the man's back. Ricky took a swing at Nero.

"I'll get you kids for this!" Nero shouted. "I'll——"

As the man raised his arm to hit the boy, another voice shouted, "You'll do nothing of the kind!" With this a fist shot out and hit Nero on the point of the chin. The fellow's knees sagged, and he sprawled onto the dusty ground.

"Dad!" Pete shouted. And added admiringly, "What a wallop!"

"Looks as if we got here just in time," Mr. Hollister said, smiling. As he spoke two policemen hurried up, followed by Mrs. Hollister and the three girls.

The officers took charge of Professor Mars and Nero, who would not talk. But Pete said, "They admitted everything to Ricky and me."

"Fine," said one of the officers.

By this time other circus people had crowded around, and when the Hollisters told them of the poodle thefts, they cried out angrily.

"We've felt all along there was something phony about these fellows," one of the aerialists said. "And we feel certain Wizard isn't being run on the level. That man Toto at Sunshine is in partnership with the owner here. Toto's been getting every-body to leave Peppo by promising them more money at Wizard. But we haven't been paid a cent yet."

"That's right," said another. "If Peppo would take me back, I'd go in a minute."

"Oh, he will," Pam spoke up. "Peppo wants you all."

"Then let's go!" said the sword swallower and the others cried, "Yes, yes!"

The Hollisters were very happy about the out-come and could hardly wait to get back to Treasure Cove with the good news. As the prisoners were led away, the children obtained leashes for the four poodles and took the dogs to the Hollisters' car. When they rode off, several performers shouted, "Hurray for the Hollisters!" The children waved gaily.

Upon reaching town, the family had breakfast

and the restaurant owner gave the animals food, too. When the Hollisters came outside, they saw a big bus parked behind their station wagon. In it were all the circus people who had deserted Peppo.

"We're going back with you!" one said.

"Swell!" Pete replied.

It was a happy ride back to Circus Island. Reaching it, the children stopped for just a moment at the motel to leave Champion in Pam's room and to return Fifi and Mimi to the Blakes. The couple were overjoyed.

Then with the Hollisters leading the way everyone trouped across the causeway. The gateman's mouth fell open when he saw his former friends.

"Peppo! Peppo! Come here quick!" he shouted.

As Peppo, Kit, and Rita ran from their house-

Nappy raced to his master.

182

boat, Pam, who was holding Nappy, let him go. The dog raced to his master and excitedly put his forepaws against the clown's chest. At the same time the sword swallower announced, "We're back to stay, Peppo!"

The clown was so overcome with joy that for a time he could not speak. Rita and Kit, meantime, hugged the Hollister children and jumped up and down with delight. Finally their father welcomed the circus performers and asked them to take their old quarters. Then he shook the Hollisters' hands.

"I'll never be able to thank you enough for all you've done," he said. "But please come back to Circus Island this evening. We'll have a celebration, and I mean a real celebration!"

"We will! We will!" the children promised.

When the Hollisters returned to the island at eight o'clock, they were greeted by the blaring of bugles. The circus band struck up a jolly tune, and Peppo greeted them in costume, his face painted in a big smile. Underneath the paint the children could see that he was wearing a real smile as well.

"Welcome! Welcome, my friends!" he said. "Tonight we are previewing this year's Sunshine Circus just for you."

The Hollisters were led into the Big Top where other clowns capered about, tumblers tumbled, and aerialists swung high above them on their trapezes.

"The best seats in the house for the folks from

Shoreham," Kit grinned as he took them to the front row.

Before the show began, Peppo ran up and stood in front of his guests. "Happy Hollisters," he said, "I can never thank you enough for all you've done for me and my children. Now I shall not have to sell my houseboat. But I have found a very good one for your customer, Mr. Hollister."

"Splendid!" said the children's father.

"Although I could never repay your kindness," Peppo went on, "there's one thing I can promise."

"What's that?" Ricky asked expectantly.

"This circus will be in Shoreham the end of June," Peppo said. "You and all your friends are invited to see our show free."

"Hurray! Hurray!" the children shouted.

Just then the trumpets sounded again. The ringmaster strode to the center ring, and the big show especially for the Happy Hollisters began!